Praise for

Nikki McCoy

Exciting, loaded with action and filled with surprises...
Nikki McCoy has penned a book that should be highly
recommended for those of us who love stories with
paranormal aspects, MM loving and suspenseful action...
 ~ *Ecata Reviews*

Total-E-Bound Publishing books by Nikki McCoy:

Keepers of the Gods
Son of Death
Master of Wrath

My Forever
Everything That You Are

EVERYTHING THAT YOU ARE

NIKKI McCOY

Everything That You Are
ISBN # 978-0-85715-774-4
©Copyright Nikki McCoy 2011
Cover Art by April Martinez ©Copyright June 2011
Interior text design by Claire Siemaszkiewicz
Total-E-Bound Publishing

Published in 2012 by Total-E-Bound Publishing, Think Tank, Ruston Way, Lincoln, LN6 7FL, United Kingdom.

EVERYTHING THAT YOU ARE

Dedication

To my wonderful husband and beautiful mom, who
showed me that true love encompasses all that we are…
And my kids, who went against their rambunctious nature
and were actually quiet for me during the
making of this book!

Prologue

Michael followed his friend into the nightclub and immediately cringed at the assault on his senses. Loud music blared from speakers placed strategically into the corner panels of each wall. The air was cool but held the scents of alcohol, tobacco, and too many desperate bodies squeezed together, trying to find release, if only for a few hours.

The crowd was full of both young and middle-aged gay and lesbian people, which surprised Michael. He'd expected to find nothing but a bunch of spoilt brats with too much of their parents' money to know what to do with.

Nick had insisted on celebrating Michael's ascension within the pack with a little bit of 'sexual variety', as he had so delicately put it the week before. Apparently, Michael's stale sex life of heterosexual one-night stands with no emotional involvement was getting to the man, although why, he had no idea.

Nick was determined to see if the reason for his emotional detachment was because he hadn't been looking in the right places...or at the right sex. What Nick didn't understand was that not only did Michael need to find a female to have pups with, but he also wasn't ready to be tied down in a relationship yet, even if he had just been proclaimed the new Alpha of his pack.

Kids and chains and further obligations could come later. For now, he was going to enjoy his freedom a little longer. Tonight, however, he would go along with his friend's antics, if for no other reason than to indulge him.

He walked with Nick to the bar, ignoring the lust-filled glances of men as he passed by them. He did, however, notice several attractive women he wouldn't mind taking home for the night. Unfortunately, they were wrapped around other females he didn't think would be open to sharing.

"Beer?" Nick yelled over the rumbling blast of music as he flagged down the bartender. With their advanced hearing, it wasn't necessary for them to compete with the blare of the noise around them to hear one another, but it was a human bar, and such things were the norm in these places.

"Make it a scotch. I have a feeling you're going to try to get me laid tonight and I'm not sure I want to be completely sober for it."

Nick shot him a devilish grin and ordered the drinks before saying, "Has a guy caught your eye already?"

Michael snorted. "No, but I'll bet plenty have caught yours."

Nick laughed and introduced him to a couple of his friends who were sitting socialising around the bar, then paid for their drinks and led them to one of the open tables lined up against the far wall. Michael finished his drink in one gulp and flagged down a waitress for another before casting his gaze out over the sea of undulating bodies crowding the dance floor.

He tried to keep track of the couples that came over to greet Nick, and politely blew off the few men brave enough to ignore his air of nonchalance and approach him for a dance. After a while, he began to lose interest. He had long ago decided the whole club dating scenario was a bit too tedious for his tastes. He much preferred his partners to come to him.

That's when he saw them. In two large cages with wide-spaced bars, suspended from either side of the ceiling at the far end of the club, were a man and a woman dancing almost obscenely to the rhythmic beat of the music. Their movements were graceful and hypnotic, but it was the man in the cage to his left that caught his attention. His lithe form moved like liquid and the definition of his toned muscles was clear to see even from this distance.

The transparent mesh shirt that ended at his abs and black, leather shorts were adorned with chains that crisscrossed his chest and thighs and emphasised the wide expanses of pale skin that were showing. Michael realised he was holding his breath, much like he had while watching professional ice-skating or the ballet on the occasions his mom had tried to force culture on him.

He slowly let the air from his lungs and felt the hardening of his cock as he continued to be riveted.

The man was captivating.

And Michael was hardly the only one to notice. There was a small gathering of men surrounding the base of the cage, which hovered about three feet from the ground. The younger ones were trying to emulate his moves while casting furtive glances his way. The older ones were either swaying slightly or not bothering to move at all as they blatantly ogled the young dancer.

Michael hadn't realised how caught up he'd become in the scene until he started at the feel of a hand on his elbow. He turned to see Nick with a knowing smirk on his face.

"We're here to take advantage of the available people, not the sexy advertisements on display."

Michael managed to pull his gaze away from the spectacle long enough to give his friend a confused look and ask, "The advertisements?"

Nick looked back over to the figure in the cage Michael had just been transfixed by and grinned. "Yeah. Those people up there get paid to dance and attract the crowd that comes in here every night looking for sex on a stick. I gotta say, though, that guy does his job very well."

Michael had already focussed his stare back on the man, who was now kneeling down to unhook the bottom latch of the door to the cage. "Yeah, he does. Where is he going?"

Nick pointed to a taller man just as scantily dressed as the first and said, "The dancers take shifts, and I think the one inside is being relieved for the moment."

They watched as the guy slipped his body to the floor in one fluid movement then held the door open as the next dancer leant down to whisper something in his ear before hoisting himself up and into the cage. The first man nodded his head and closed the door, making sure the latch was in place.

Michael watched as he was groped by several men on his way to an alcove between two pillars behind a grouping of loveseats. The back area was designed to give couples a modicum of privacy while they made out. It became clear that the dancer was trying to find his own solitude when he nimbly dodged the grasping hands of his admirers.

At least three men clustered around the man as he bent down to pick up a bottle of water from the floor. He'd only managed two swallows before one of his more insistent followers tugged at his arm, causing the liquid in his hand to spill down his chest and soak the front of his shorts. The other two men laughed as the dancer bowed his head in embarrassment.

A change of songs brought on a shift in the crowd and Michael's view of the young man was temporarily obscured. He was tempted to get up and move to a place with a better vantage point, but didn't want to make his intentions too obvious to Nick. For the few frustrating minutes it took for the cluster of gyrating bodies to dissipate from in front of him, he pondered what it was about this man that caught his attention so.

Nothing about him should have appealed to Michael. He liked his partners to have at least a medium-sized build, be strong-willed...and female! From his willowy stature to his acceptance of being bullied by others larger than him—which seemed to be just about everyone—he was the exact opposite of what Michael was looking for in a mate.

Let alone a fuck-bunny for the night.

And yet he couldn't help but zero in on the small man as soon as his view was clear. Though several yards separated them, his keen eyesight allowed him to clearly see a beefy beau wrap his hand around the dancer's arm so tightly that there was an almost imperceptible blanching of colour from his lips.

The larger man withdrew something from the front pocket of his slacks and pressed it into the dancer's hand before lowering his head to whisper in his ear. The other guy jerked his head down in acquiescence but wrenched his arm away before heading to a back door with a red exit sign over it.

Michael had a pretty good idea of what was going on and was about to turn away when the dancer suddenly lifted his head to stare straight at him. His equilibrium instantly took a dive as the flashing lights and annoying clamour of all those around him took a back seat to the vision of that face. It was clear and guarded all at once...and then it was gone.

The back door was slammed shut after he was pulled through it and Nick's insistent voice was barking in Michael's ear, demanding his attention over something he was too shaken to concentrate on.

Finally, his friend's voice took on a concerned, low tone that shook him out of his sudden trance and he turned to the other man dazedly.

"Michael, are you okay? Is there a threat here I should know about?"

Michael gave himself a mental shake and forcibly focussed his awareness back on his surroundings. Along with his own promotion within the ranks of their clan, Nick had been appointed as one of his Betas. It wouldn't do to get him worked up over nothing. At least he thought it was nothing.

One too many shots in an atmosphere practically oozing sex and fornication. Damn, he needed to get laid.

"Sorry, think I should stick to beers from now on. I'm getting too old for this shit," he replied. Nick let out a whoop of laughter and slapped him on the back, calling him a lousy liar and accusing him of being amorously taken with one of the pretty boys in the club, in none such elegant words. Michael refused to think of how close to the truth he really was.

The next hour was one of the longest in Michael's life. As the patrons got drunker, the come-on lines got tackier, until eventually he thought he would kill something if he didn't get out of there soon. The fact that the dancer he had locked gazes with hadn't reappeared, or that he couldn't get the man out of his head, had nothing to do with his increasingly foul mood.

Not a damn thing.

He just needed to get home, get laid, and concentrate on tomorrow and all of the duties that came along with his new position.

Nick must have sensed his building impatience, because he stood up then and bid farewell to the lesbian couple he'd been chatting with. Michael gladly followed his lead and threw a few bills onto the table for the last of their drinks before winding his way towards the front door.

By the way people immediately cleared a path for him instead of flocking to him, he guessed that he wore his aggravation on his face a little too clearly, but that didn't bother him in the least. An image had been burnt into his mind's eye and, no matter how hard he tried, he couldn't get rid of it.

Once they were outside, he took in a lungful of clean, crisp night air with a little too much relish.

Nick laughed and said, "It can't have been all that bad. I saw at least ten numbers make their way across the table to you. Plan on putting any of them to use?"

Michael grunted and continued to walk across the street to where his friend's car was parked. There had been considerably more than ten numbers, and not all from men.

"Maybe. I've always wanted to be in a threesome. How about you?"

Nick just sent him a disgusted glare and mumbled under his breath, "Lucky bastard," along with a few other choice words. Michael chuckled, feeling his mood lighten already. Any chance he got to best his friend in one of their many private competitions made his day. Nick was his equal in almost every factor, and in the areas where one was lacking, the other excelled. It created a balance that had worked to their advantage since they were kids.

Michael was well aware of the fact that if Nick had opted for the position of Alpha, it would have been a close call between the two of them, but he felt in no way threatened. He would support his friend as much as Nick had always supported him in anything they set their minds to. It was the main reason he had appointed the man his Beta.

He heard the soft click of the locks being released inside Nick's silver BMW moments before a rustling a little too close to his left had him whirling around, crouching into a loose fighter's stance. Shock momentarily seized his body as recognition of the man standing a few yards away hit. It took several seconds for him to loosen his muscles enough to straighten his body.

It was the dancer. He was sure of it. But this man didn't look like a man at all. He couldn't have been more than seventeen, eighteen years old, if that. In human years, that might amount to adulthood, but it was plain now that this man was a shifter, which made him all of a pup.

There was a faint, strange smell to him, though, that was foreign to Michael. He swiftly closed the distance between them and leant forward until his face hovered above the crease where the man's neck met his shoulder, not missing the slight flinch, and inhaled. The smell of the ocean, wild flowers and something else hit him hard, causing him to reel back in confusion. Arousal slammed into him with a force that made him gasp. His cock quickly stood to attention and tried to fight its way through the zipper of his pants in an almost painful reaction.

The features of the man suddenly struck him with crystal clarity. His hair was platinum blond and created a shroud about his face that made him look close to angelic. His eyes were such a deep blue that they appeared purple in the dim light surrounding the parking lot. His red, wide lips were parted slightly, giving Michael a glimpse of small, gleaming teeth that had him licking his own for want of a taste of the gorgeous mouth.

His world narrowed to the vision of this smaller being in front of him, until he was all Michael could see and smell. *This is my mate!* The certainty of that thought was as undeniable as the knowledge that the sun would rise in the morning.

A low growl coming from inside the car distracted him from his appraisal and he turned to see Nick leaning over from the driver's side seat to stare at the boy with a harsh look on his face. "That's that little dancer who whores himself out to every desperate john in the club on his breaks. You saw him earlier. Come on, Michael. He's hot — but nothing but trash."

That statement angered Michael, but he had no reason to doubt his friend. He'd never visited the bar he and Nick had just come from, and therefore knew nothing of the people who worked there. Not to mention the fact that he'd witnessed a questionable exchange earlier between the dancer and another man.

As he looked down at the shame-filled yet hopeful expression of the boy, however, his desire beat through him so fiercely that it took his breath away.

Myriad emotions tore through his chest. Fear of what his clan might think. Shame at throwing away his mother's hope for grandchildren. Confusion as to why Mother Earth would choose a male mate for him.

"I'm sorry," he whispered. "I can't do this right now."

The boy frowned and took a hesitant step forward but Michael quickly span around. Seating himself inside the vehicle, he told Nick to start driving in a voice so gruff he almost didn't recognise it as his own. He didn't even realise that his hands were shaking until it took him three tries to buckle his seatbelt.

Nick cast covert glances at him with a concerned look on his face but Michael was too wound up to offer an excuse for his unusual behaviour. Doubts swirled like wildfire and he struggled to analyse the situation as he did all others, by weighing the pros and cons.

Five minutes into the trip home, he wanted to yell at Nick to turn the car around, but he bit his tongue. He needed time to digest this new information. The dancer worked at the club, which meant he should be there the following night. That gave Michael at least a twenty-four hour window to get his head and his hormones under control.

At least that's what he repeated to himself.

By the time Nick pulled into Michael's driveway some thirty minutes later to drop him off, though, he couldn't take it anymore. The cherubic features and longing expression in the man's eyes plagued his mind, along with the crushed look on his face when Michael had refused him.

"We need to go back. Now."

Nick paused in confusion. "Did you leave something there?"

A desperate burst of laughter escaped Michael's lips. "You could say that. My pride. My sanity, and something a hell of a lot more important."

"What the hell are you talking about?"

"Just trust me. I need to get back to that club." He locked gazes with Nick, imploring with his eyes.

Another half an hour later, Nick pulled into the same parking lot and Michael was out of the car before it stopped rolling. He could still detect the scent of his mate but it was overpowered by that of another shifter. Not giving up hope, he tracked, sniffed and asked about any trace of the dancer, but after an hour, he'd found nothing.

Cold dread invaded his body and clung to his heart with a vice-like grip. He didn't believe in once-in-a-lifetime chances, but he couldn't shake the feeling that he'd blown his.

Once again at his house, he managed to give Nick an absent thanks and weak smile. "Guess I'll have to find it another time." There was no way he could divulge his shame to his friend. "I'll see you tomorrow, okay?"

He didn't wait for a reply before climbing out of the car and slamming the door closed. He felt his face flame a little when he noticed that Nick refused to drive off until he saw him inside his house. He must look more shaken than he thought. He walked through the dark interior of his house, not bothering to turn the lights on, having no need of them thanks to his wolf's eyesight, and went straight to the kitchen to pour a full glass of bourbon.

Walking back out to his living room, he turned his body slowly in a full circle, taking in the comfort and majesty of his elaborate yet modest home. He tried to pretend that the dancer he had met earlier tonight piqued his interest only because he had seemed so effeminate. And it was the truth—his features had been so delicate that if it weren't for his flat chest and the bulge in his shorts, he could easily have been mistaken for a female. But the sick, gut-wrenching loss that permeated from within called his bluff.

Tomorrow. Tomorrow he would find him and to hell with the consequences.

* * * *

Kaden collapsed to his knees on the gravel of the parking lot and watched the car as it made its way down the street and took the only person he'd ever been attracted to away from him. The momentary glimpse of him in the club had mesmerised Kaden and he had soaked up every detail of those striking features before being rudely yanked out of the back door.

The man had shoulder-length hair so black that it had shone under the flashing lights in the club, and his body was massive yet trim. It was his glowing, hazel eyes, however, that had held Kaden captive.

The john hadn't taken it well when Kaden had given him back his money for the blowjob he'd agreed to give, but he didn't take the hard shove and cruel words he'd received personally. He just couldn't get the image of the stranger out of his mind. He'd wanted desperately to run back into the club and find out if the huge arms on that man would hold him as tightly as he imagined, but didn't want to risk being approached by another john.

Up close, the man had seemed so handsome and smelt so good that he'd been robbed of words. For that one brief moment in time, his hopes had soared…then been slaughtered in the next. The pain of the man's rejection had been confusing at first, a shock to his system, and the longer he knelt there, the more intense the feelings of hurt and abandonment became.

He didn't understand the cacophony of agonising emotions filling him and they soon became more than he could bear. He doubled over as his chest constricted in racking, sharp pains that quickly spread throughout his body, threatening to consume him if he didn't retain his grip on reality.

A low-pitched, keening wail pierced his ears, drilling into his skull until there was nothing but that horrid sound reverberating throughout his head. After a while, his throat became so sore that he had to force it closed, only then realising that the wailing had been coming from him.

Despair filled every cavity of his being until he was nothing but an empty shell, and still he couldn't understand the feelings coursing through him. A gentle caress on his right shoulder had him lurching sideways in his effort to get away from whoever had discovered him in his moment of weakness.

"It's okay, boy. I won't hurt you," a voice said. It was deep and commanding, and Kaden felt drawn to raise his eyes to look upon the intruder. This man could easily be the same height and build of the man who had just deserted him. His frame was large and imposing, but the streetlamp behind him backlit his features, making his face hard to discern.

Kaden still felt empty, battered, and knew there was no way he could bring himself to perform tonight, despite the fact that he needed the money. He didn't want to return home and risk his mom and sister seeing him like this, but there was nowhere else to go.

He slowly got to his hands and knees, feeling as if he had aged forty years, and said, "Sorry man, I'm done in the club for the night. Find another entertainer." His voice caught on that last word as he remembered the look of fear on the face of the man he had risked his last vestiges of pride for. Hopelessness threatened to take what will he had left to him as he got to his feet and headed blindly for the street.

A hard hand clamped onto his shoulder and span him around. Before he could even react, another hand gripped his throat in a hold so tight he saw black spots dancing before his eyes in seconds. A torrent of sickening emotions lit his body on fire until he thought he would pass out. Hate and lust and greed pounded into his mind mercilessly, with such force that this new pain superceded his own.

His scream was cut off before it could even reach his lips.

"Unlike you, I don't take rejection so well," the stranger said. Kaden tried to struggle but the man pulled him against his hard body and released his shoulder to lock his arm around Kaden's torso and arms in a vice so strong it was all he could do to keep air in his lungs.

He was half-carried to the far right corner of the parking lot, into a narrow opening between two buildings, then slammed face-forward into a wall.

By this time, he was so desperate for air that when the man loosened his grip on his neck, he could do nothing but gulp down great breaths. He could feel the much larger body pressed against his entire length, the stranger's cock jutting into his backside almost like a promise, or threat. Hot, alcohol-laced breath fanned across his cheek from behind as he heard the man say, "What clan are you from?"

Oh shit! How could I not have noticed?

He'd known the man he had approached earlier was a wolf — had been taught to recognise their scent by his father so many years ago — but he had been too wrapped up in his misery to take note of this one. Kaden would have laughed at his stupidity had he not just been spurned by the only man whose attraction actually meant a damn to him, though he had not the slightest clue why.

He had to get the man's flesh off his own. There was no way he could battle the other's raging emotions and physical strength at the same time. Although he had to admit he wasn't even close to his match in sheer brawn.

"I have no clan..." He felt himself yanked back, only to be slammed again into the brick wall in front of him. Pain blossomed in his head and chest and his cry was choked off. Real terror began to flood his body on top of the disgusting feelings of the other man, and his thoughts scattered into fragments.

"Coven, then? I can smell the mage in you. The truth, boy, or I will cut your tongue out," the man sneered. Kaden tried to concentrate on his words, but fear had already replaced coherent thought.

"P—please. I don't know." He swallowed as a hand once again clamped down fiercely around his throat, and tried desperately to think of something the man wanted to hear. "No coven. No clan. I have n—nothing..." Suddenly, he was whirled around and felt the iron grip of the stranger disappear.

Kaden somehow managed to lock his knees to keep himself from falling, but instead of looking around to find an escape route like he knew he should be doing, he glanced up at the stranger and found himself frozen in stark terror.

The man was rubbing his cock through his pants and sliding his gaze lewdly over Kaden's body. The look in his eyes when they finally caught and held Kaden's kept him immobile. They were crazed and feral, but it was the intelligence behind them that shone through the most.

That was never a good combination.

"Pretty," the stranger said as one corner of his mouth lifted up into a smile that didn't reach his eyes. "Yes, I think I'll take you home." Just as Kaden found the courage to run, he felt an iron fist strike the side of his head and heard the sharp crack of his skull hitting the wall behind him before the world fell away.

Chapter One

Four years later…

Michael stared blankly at the computer screen before him. It contained the same emailed response he'd received from countless other Alphas spanning a nearly thousand-mile radius from his hometown of West Plains, Missouri. The words were different but the message was always the same.

Alpha Michael Rockheim,
I am sorry to inform you that I have no young man fitting the description you gave living amongst my clan. My Betas have searched the surrounding area to no avail. I have alerted my community to report any possible sightings immediately and will let you know if any useful information turns up.
Good luck to you.
Sincerely,
Alpha James Sternberg

The words were beginning to blur together as he read it for the fifth time, his heart refusing to accept that his mind was veering towards defeat. He thought back to that excruciating time that had followed his chance encounter with his mate and once again cursed himself for being such a fool.

The pain of his mistake had cut so deeply at first that he couldn't bring himself to confide in anyone for six months. In the end, however, it had been the bond of love his parents shared that had broken him.

He recalled that evening spent over dinner at their house with perfect clarity. He'd always known that his parents' love for each other was matched only by their love for him. That night, watching them perform all of their familiar rituals such as a caress at the table, a kiss stolen when they thought he wasn't looking, only succeeded in driving home the pain of knowing that he might never have that kind of connection to another, thanks to his rash behaviour and fear of the unknown.

It was while his mother was cutting slices of peach pie for dessert, leaning into the kiss his father placed on her temple, that she had turned to notice the silent tears streaming down his cheeks.

She had dropped the knife and let it clatter to the floor in her rush to pull him into a hug and ask what was wrong. He'd looked at her in confusion until she wiped away a tear from his cheek that he hadn't even realised was there.

A flush that he was sure covered his entire body had rushed through him at the thought of being caught crying by his mom. He was more scared at that point than he had ever been in his life, because he knew he couldn't lie to his parents, which meant that he would have to come clean. Both about his mate and his shame at rejecting him.

Michael had cleared his throat and spoken in a low voice. "Mom." Then turning to his father, "Dad, I think I'm gay." He'd held his breath, waiting for the denials and accusations that were sure to come, and they did, but not in the form he had expected. His dad's face had remained stoical as the older man's eyes searched his, but it was his mom that had spoken up first, or rather shouted.

"That's what this is about? You've been moping around for the past *six* months, then come here and get so upset that you're crying because you think we'll...what?...hate you for being gay? Michael Nathaniel Rockheim, I ought to bend you over my knee right now. How could you possibly think that your father and I would be so callous as to turn you away simply because of your sexual preferences? Boy, I should just take you outside and whip your hide till…"

His mom had continued to berate and threaten him thoroughly as she retrieved the fallen knife, washed it, and continued to cut slices of pie for everyone. Michael had been so dumbfounded that he had started to laugh. That is, until he had seen the look of hurt in his father's eyes.

"I'm sorry," he'd said, cutting into his mom's angry tirade. "I really didn't mean to offend you. I just knew how much you wanted grandchildren and…"

"Baby," his mom had pleaded in a tortured voice, "how could you possibly think that I would trade your happiness for mine? Especially when there are more ways than one to have children."

Shame had flooded him anew at his wrongful assumptions.

"So...you're not upset that I might be gay?" His mother had raised the knife still in her hand, pointing it at him with a glare in her eyes that bespoke pain, lots of pain, if he didn't stop with the apparent insults.

He had quickly held up his hands in surrender and this time couldn't keep the laugh of relief from bubbling up from his chest. "Okay, okay. Truly sorry here," he said with a chuckle. The honesty and love his parents were showing him, despite the fact that he knew they'd both been looking forward to having grandchildren, humbled him in a way that nothing else had.

"Son, of course we have no problem with you being gay, but what exactly did you mean when you said you *think* you might be gay? Something tells me this is a lot more serious than a simple experiment."

He had known his father would have picked up on that little detail—it was the mark of a true Alpha, one which he himself had used to his own benefit for many years. Still, he had cringed at the thought of having to admit to his parents the extent of the disastrous choice of rejecting his mate.

Hesitantly, he'd said, "I'd never been attracted to a man until I met him. My mate. It was about six months ago, but he was barely a pup at the time. Maybe eighteen. I got so scared that I left him. He was...he...shit, he was working in a club, Dad, as a dancer, and I think doing something on the side for extra money."

His father's face was once again stoical, while his mother had wiped briskly at her eyes as if to hide tears.

"Honey, if that young man was working underage in a club, then he was probably doing the only thing he knew how to survive. Oh Michael, you've got to find him. He's obviously without a clan. That poor thing could be taken advantage of without any kind of protection. Oh sweetheart...he must be so lost." Right then, seeing the tears of sympathy in his mom's eyes for a man she didn't even know except for the fact that he was her son's mate, he'd felt like the biggest ass on the planet.

A sharp knock at the door brought him out of his reverie and he glanced at the wall clock next to his desk. Quarter to one. It would be his dad bringing over the CD of spreadsheets for Mrs O'Neily's lands. She was looking to extend her acres to include a part of the Buckland's orchards, which they had agreed to exchange with her for rights to several of her well-springs so that they could feed their crops with less expense.

"Come in," he yelled, still unable to take his eyes off the latest email attesting to his failed attempts to find his mate. Though his office was located beyond his living room and down a long hallway, he was still able to pick up his father's distinct scent and hear the soft click of the latch as he entered his home and closed the door behind him. Michael rubbed the bridge of his nose between his thumb and forefinger.

"No luck yet?" his father asked as he eased himself down into a leather recliner positioned to the side of the desk. Michael glanced at the man who could have been his twin but for a sprinkling of grey hair and a few additional laughter lines around the edges of his eyes.

He didn't have to ask to know what he was talking about. The evidence of his failed search was staring him in the face. He knew he should get back to work, but the hopelessness of the situation was wearing on him. It had been four years since he'd started his search for his mate, using several channels to get hold of every clan he could reach, and even some he hadn't known about, thanks to his father. But it had all been in vain.

Michael sighed heavily and dropped his head into his hands, his elbows resting on the desktop. "Dad, I left him out there. Alone. I was afraid just because he had a penis between his legs."

He was vaguely embarrassed to be so vulgar in front of his father, but the older man was the only one he could talk to about this. He hadn't mentioned the discovery of his mate to anyone else in his clan, and discussing sex with his mother was *not* an option.

Sam reached over and placed a gentle hand on his shoulder in support. "Son, we'll find him. Don't give up."

Michael laughed bitterly at that and shook off his father's hand as he stood up and began pacing the room. "You don't know that. A mate is the most precious gift one can receive from Mother Earth, and I spurned him. I took her gift and threw it away like so much trash."

That familiar ache that he had come to live with every minute of every day began to gnaw at his insides, threatening to take over his self-control. He stopped his pacing beside the window behind the loveseat in his office, staring at the beautiful landscape spreading out before him in ravines and rolling hills filled with trees bursting with life. It was hard to look upon such peaceful surroundings when his entire being was filled with turmoil and regret.

He didn't even notice that his father had stood up until he felt a sharp tug on the ponytail at the back of his neck. "Stop what you're thinking right now. He isn't dead and you will find him. Damn, you're just like you were at the age of ten. Too damned impatient for your own good and wanting Mother Earth to serve you everything on a silver platter. You made a mistake, son, and you're working to rectify it. You will find him."

His father's sage words rang through him, and he knew that he was reaching the end of his patience, but what else was there to do? The idea of giving up the search for his mate was inconceivable. He let out a sigh and grasped his father's hand on his shoulder, giving it a squeeze to let him know that he understood.

Returning to his desk, he was about to ask his father for the disk containing Mrs O'Neily's spreadsheets when his cell phone went off. He kept two with him at all times. His private phone, which only his parents and Betas had access to, and one the rest of the clan was directed to use to contact him. The caller ID on his private line identified Nick, his Beta and long-time friend, and he answered it immediately, knowing the man only used this line for business.

"Nick, what's up?"

"I was just out here surveying Mrs O'Neily's lands for you and got pulled into a conversation with Wiley and Buckland and they've all expressed concern over the whereabouts of Stephen McCain. You remember him?"

Michael knew instantly the man he was referring to. Stephen had been caught a few times transporting illegal drugs to other clans but they had never been able to convict him of selling them. Most clans tended to live on the outskirts of human society, if not completely away from it. Some members saw this as an opportunity to take advantage of the privacy and land to grow drugs and sell them to humans or other clan members to make a profit.

Michael was far from fond of Stephen, but the man was still a member of his community, and he was therefore responsible for his wellbeing.

"Yeah, I remember him. What has he gotten himself into this time?"

Nick grunted. "Well, that's just it. No one knows. Buckland and Wiley remarked that they haven't seen him in almost a week, and Mrs O'Neily is telling me that he seemed pretty scared the last time she saw him. Thought someone might be after him or something."

Michael barely sucked in the sarcastic remark dancing on the tip of his tongue before taking a breath and saying, "Fine. Have you checked out his place yet?"

"Yeah. No forced entries and nothing out of the ordinary inside, if you take into account the man's disgusting living habits. Do you know I had to walk through weeks-old, half-filled pizza boxes and underwear? Seriously, man, if you don't enforce a law against that kind of nasty, sick, disgusting..."

"I get the picture," Michael cut him off before he could actually get the full picture from Nick's descriptions.

Nick grunted again and grudgingly continued with his report. "Well, anyway, it looks like the guy took off. I don't think this is one of his usual drug-run attempts, though, because his cell phone, stash, and car are still there. Much as I hate to admit it, I think our little criminal might have finally gotten into more trouble than he could handle."

Michael glanced over at his father, knowing he had heard every word of the conversation. His dad had a tight-lipped, grim expression on his face and nodded, telling Michael that this situation did indeed call for a search party. He squeezed his eyes shut, knowing that he couldn't put off this search. He'd already been neglecting some of his duties as Alpha in his search for his mate. He had to take care of the business at hand first.

"Call Joseph. We'll meet in one hour at Stephen's apartment to pick up his trail. Have Dennis question anyone else Stephen might have talked to or been around before he left. See if he can't dig up anything on our favourite criminal." Michael hung up the phone after getting Nick's customary grunt of assent, then turned back to his dad. There was a look of apprehension on his face that made Michael nervous. "What are you thinking?"

"I've just got a strange feeling about this hunt." Sam lived by his instincts, just as he had taught him to do, so if his father was having misgivings about the situation, Michael wasn't about to ignore them. "Do what you have to do, but I want you to be careful on this one." He dropped the CD on his desk and stood up.

Sam made sure to catch his son's gaze to emphasise his point. "Contact me in no more than two days. After that, I'll send out my own search party."

His father was out of his office and closing the front door to his house before he could question his cryptic warning. Michael was a seasoned tracker and fighter, as were all three of his Betas. They had learnt from the best, having had all of their fathers as trainers and Sam's personal Betas as instructors as well, so for his father to warn him about a simple find-and-recovery mission didn't bode well for him or his men.

* * * *

"Jade! You done with them horses yet?"

Kaden had long since become used to responding to the name Jade, which he had given himself in order to keep his identity hidden. He cringed at the rough, Texan accent of Jim, one of the seasonal stable hands.

He leaned in to the firm flank of Mockingbird, wanting to disappear into her strong muscles and absorb some of the mare's strength into his own body, but he knew that was impossible. Just as he knew that Jim wouldn't stop harassing him until he was acknowledged.

Kaden pushed away from Mockingbird's quivering flesh, not wanting more of his nervousness to be projected into the horse's gentle being, and filled her bail with oats before exiting her stall.

He kept his head lowered, hoping that by some miracle Jim wouldn't notice him, and continued on to the front of the stable house to oil the harnesses and saddles. By this time, the rest of the workers had gathered in the main house for the evening meal.

The swagger of Jim's footsteps behind him was unmistakable and he tensed his body against the unwanted advances he knew were coming.

Without fail, he felt Jim's body crash into his from behind, forcing him against the hardwood planks lining the tack room of the stable. The acceleration of his breathing threatened hyperventilation, but he kept that in check the way he always did, reminding himself that this was nowhere near the worst of his experiences.

The hard length of Jim's cock pressed against his buttocks, ratcheting his fear up another notch.

"I asked you a question, boy."

Kaden felt bile rise as Jim's chew-laced breath fanned over his neck. The man had never been so bold before, keeping his innuendos and advances to gropes and lewd comments in the past.

Kaden let his body go pliant and looked to his right, searching for some object he could use in his defence, thankful that none of the man's bare skin was touching his, yet.

Jim pressed his body closer, swivelling his hips and massaging his cock against Kaden's backside in anticipation of his plans, which Kaden had no delusions about. The man had been threatening to take him since Kaden had first arrived at the ranch almost a year ago, but Jim was only seasonal whereas Kaden was a full-time employee. The season was about to end, which meant that this was probably Jim's last opportunity to make good on his promises.

Kaden seized what little courage he had and veered to his left. Grabbing the nearest harness hanging from the hooks on the wall he was pressed against, he used his momentum to swing it towards the face of his assailant. Jim, however, was surprisingly more agile than he had given the man credit for, and dodged the makeshift weapon, reciprocating with a vicious strike to Kaden's temple. A sea of stars swam into Kaden's vision and he landed in a heap on the hard-packed earthen floor.

For a few terrifying moments, he could only register the callused hands fumbling at the buttons of his pants and wrenching them down, along with his underwear, to expose his ass. He twisted onto his back and curled his hands into fists before swinging them at any part of the man straddling him that he could come into contact with.

Another bash to the same side of his head momentarily ended his defence and he squeezed his eyes shut against the spinning of the room. Those grasping hands flipped him back over and the blunt tip of Jim's cock pressed against his crack.

Suddenly, Kaden felt the air shift behind him and heard sounds of fighting, but this time they didn't involve him. He rolled to his side and quickly pulled up his pants, blinking away tears. Jim might try to attack him again, but he couldn't keep lying there in such a vulnerable state.

He kept his eyes closed against the merciless pounding in his head, wondering if it would fall off if he moved too fast, and curled into himself on the ground. After a minute, he became aware of the silence ringing in his ears and a figure kneeling over him. When he felt the cool touch of fingers at the lump on the side of his head, he couldn't keep a small whimper from escaping.

"It's okay, son. He won't be laying a hand on you ever again. Let me see your face."

He knew that voice. It was gentle yet gravelly and held a wealth of authority he'd come to admire during his time on the ranch.

Oh no. Anyone but him. Kaden cracked open his lids and peered up at the face looming over his, lined with concern.

Sure enough, Henry Connel, his boss, stared down at him, or rather at the damage done to his head near his right eye. His temple throbbed with his heartbeat, and judging by the frown that now creased the older man's brow, it probably looked as bad as it felt.

If he'd been able to, he would have kicked himself for letting this happen. This was the best job he'd ever had and he had to go and ruin it by getting into trouble. It seemed inevitable with him, and usually he learnt to accept it as his fate, but this time, he truly regretted failing the older man. Henry had been nothing but kind and honest with him since taking him on.

"Come on. Let's get some ice on that shiner before it swells up any more." Henry extended his hand to help Kaden up, but he flinched away from it out of reaction. The frown on the cowboy's face deepened, and he mentally cursed himself for making the situation worse than it already was.

"That's okay, sir," he whispered, then cleared his throat. "I can manage. I'm sorry about the trouble. I can leave by tomorrow if that's..." Kaden slowly raised himself onto his hands and knees, the pounding in his head threatening to cause his stomach to retch. Fortunately, there wasn't any food in it. There normally wasn't.

"Leave! What the hell for, that piece of shit?" Henry pointed to an area of the floor just out of Kaden's sight, and he carefully swivelled his head in the direction of his boss's finger. Lying unconscious on the ground with more bruises on his face than Kaden could count was Jim. The man looked like he'd gone a round with a professional boxer.

A small smile broke out on Kaden's face and he turned back to look at his boss with a whole new level of respect. The guy may look old, with his sun-tanned, leathery face and greying hair, but damn he could pack a punch! Kaden started to laugh despite the gravity of the situation but the pain in his head quickly ended that idea.

He gradually got to his feet, using the wall for support, while Henry kept an arm out to steady him if he needed it. He refused to look again at his attacker, but the feelings of shame over what had almost happened and the anger at himself for getting into trouble again settled in his chest like stones. This wasn't the first time he'd caused 'distraction' in some of the other workers Henry employed.

"I don't want to cause you any more trouble, sir. I'll be out of your hair…"

"Boy, you didn't start any trouble. There will always be jackasses like him," he nodded to the still unconscious form of Jim lying some distance away, "thinking that they can get away with anything they want. Fortunately, there will also always be bulldogs like me to put them in their place. Besides, you're a true horse whisperer. Men like him are a dime a dozen. You, my boy, are more valuable than anyone on this ranch, my wife excluded of course."

Henry flashed him a toothy grin. "You leave now and I'll have to tan your hide, too." That managed to bring a full smile to Kaden's lips. "Besides, there's no way Cheryl would give up her little protégé. Missy's as good as the daughter she never had."

Kaden let out a breath of laughter, but when he pushed himself away from the wall, he would have toppled over again but for the swiftness of the arm rounding his waist to steady him. This time, he let his boss keep hold of him and steer him slowly out of the barn.

Henry took him up the path to the main house, bypassing the little bungalow he shared with his sister at the back, for which he was grateful. He didn't want Missy to see him like this. Before they reached the back door, though, he glanced up at his employer's grim face and said, "Sir?"

"Yeah, son?"

"Remind me never to get on your bad side."

Henry let out a deep roar of laughter and simply shook his head.

* * * *

Kaden woke up the next morning nervous, unsure of whether his boss still thought the trouble he seemed to constantly cause was worth the effort of keeping him on. Missy had seen the large bruises on the side of his face and started in with a barrage of questions he didn't know how to answer. Mrs Connel, being the saint that she was, had come to his rescue by distracting the girl with a new recipe for breakfast. They both shared a passion for cooking that went well beyond his or Henry's understanding.

His doubts were quickly squelched, however, when Jim walked into the large dining room in the main house where the farm hands and Henry were eating breakfast at the long table. Silence descended upon the room as every man there took in the colourful bruises marking Jim's face.

Kaden watched from the kitchen, where he always took his meals with Missy and Cheryl. Henry stood up and glared at the other man with a look that had everyone in the room suddenly gazing down at their plates as if they contained the seven wonders of the world.

"Pack your shit and get the hell off my ranch. I ever see you on my land again, I'll shoot you on sight," Henry said in a low, almost amiable voice that fooled no one.

Jim sputtered in indignation, then turned his head to see Kaden standing to the side of the doorway leading into the kitchen. "Boss, I didn't do nothin' wrong. You can't honestly be taking the word of a little whore who was begging me to..."

"Out!" Henry yelled. The other men sitting around the table finally looked up to take in the large bruises covering a good half of Kaden's face, to the bruising on Jim's face, then finally to the red, swollen knuckles of Henry's fists clenched at his sides.

It didn't take them long to figure out what had happened, and Kaden felt a furious blush scald his cheeks at the humiliation of seeing the realisation dawn in every man's eyes as they looked at him. He wanted to crawl into a corner and hide from the scrutiny of those he worked with, when one of the men raked his chair back against the hardwood floor to stand up.

"You sick son of a..." The man strode straight over to Jim, reared back his fist and slammed it square in the centre of Jim's nose. The sickening crack of his nose breaking filled the room, but soon after, more chairs were scraped back as more men stood.

Kaden stared, wide-eyed, as at least three other men joined the first to crowd around Jim's now hunched-over form, pushing him towards the door with the mass of their bodies. Threats rang out from the circle of men and one of them even booted Jim's ass out of the front door they had so graciously opened for him.

Kaden continued to stand, dumbfounded, in the doorway of the kitchen as the small group of men came back into the dining room and nodded to him as they sat down again to finish their meal. Henry nodded to him also, and Kaden didn't miss the look of pride in his eyes as Henry turned to look at the men who had stood up for Kaden. It had all happened so quickly that Kaden was barely able to register the intense gratitude he felt towards these men before his boss boomed out the required chores and assignments for the day.

His appetite lost, but for a good reason this time, Kaden helped Cheryl and Missy gather the dishes to be washed and put away once the men had vacated the dining room. Again, his sister tried to question him about what had happened, and again, he was saved by the careful interruptions of Mrs Connel.

Once he finished his part in assisting them, he went out to the stables to grab a saddle and harness for Mockingbird. He'd been working on her progression in high jumps and manoeuvrability for the past few weeks and she was coming along really well. Most of the horses Henry kept were for breeding and racing, but a few he wanted trained for shows and contests.

Due to her skittishness around people, Mockingbird had been slotted for breeding when Henry had bought her a month ago. Her former owner had abused her badly and she had constantly reared back at the slightest shadow or sudden movement. After days of constant gentling and soothing, Kaden had discovered a spirit in her that would have died had she not been given the chance to explore her talents with a kind hand.

Henry had been extremely reluctant to let him try to train the frightened mare, calling it a waste of valuable time. Within a week, however, Mockingbird had improved so greatly that the older man had grudgingly given his consent to allow Kaden to continue to work with her along with the other horses he trained.

Kaden knew he wasn't a real horse whisperer, and felt guilty for fooling his boss every time he received a compliment on his work. But after finding a job that enabled him to use his gift for good instead of evil, he was opposed to giving it up.

Kaden laid the mare's harness and saddle over the top of her stall wall and walked over to Mockingbird, feeling along her beautiful, sleek lines as he began to project his calming feelings into her.

After he had escaped, he'd refused to use his gift in any capacity, not even sure he could without someone touching him. It had taken him several months to discover that his mom had died shortly after his kidnapping. The solitary mage his mom had appointed to care for Missy just before her death had refused to relinquish guardianship of his sister unless Kaden could support her.

His body no longer fit for viewing, he'd remained homeless, doing everything but selling his ass to stay alive. Being out in public was out of the question He couldn't risk being found again.

A wild dog had crept up to him one night while he was sleeping against the side of a building hidden behind a pile of wooden crates. The animal smelt the refuse rotting in a trash can a few feet from him and sniffed him out to make sure he wasn't a threat. Kaden had awakened with a start to a cold nose pressed into his hand, but as soon as the dog realised he was awake, it had crouched down into a defensive position and let out a low, menacing growl.

Kaden had lain there, too afraid to move but reluctant to hurt the dog if it came to that. It had been painfully obvious that the mutt was half-starved and more afraid of losing its chance at a few sparse scraps than it was of Kaden. Its ribs were sticking out of its sides and its belly was sucked in so tight from its emptiness that Kaden couldn't even see it from his lower position on the ground.

They'd remained there, locked in their positions, neither one willing to back off, until Kaden had involuntarily sent his emotions into the dog, wanting it to know that he wasn't a threat.

He'd never forget the shock he'd felt when the mutt whined plaintively, then lowered its head to his palm to lick it. After that, it seemed like the more wonder and joy Kaden began to feel and project at being able to reach out to the lonely creature, the more the dog began to relax in his presence. It had been liberating and humbling at the same time. He had never been able to project his own emotions before then. It had always been others who projected their emotions through him.

He'd immediately thought of all the ways he could abuse his ability to communicate with animals, just as Kaden's former owner had abused his gift to take advantage of humans and the weres in his owner's clan. But he'd quickly abandoned that thought. This was different. *He* was different.

It had still taken him several days to realise that it wasn't his gift that was evil—it was the way in which he had used it, or had been forced to use it by others. For the first time in his life, he had begun to feel confident in his ability to bring about good with his power.

It wasn't until he had stumbled upon Henry's farm, however, that he'd been able to put it to use for his own personal gain and to afford to support his sister. Starved and sleep-deprived due to the harshness of the cold spring nights, Kaden had been heading for the barn in hopes of finding warm shelter for the night. Before he'd made it inside, he'd become entranced by the elegant form of a young stallion in a paddock, a stallion he later learnt Henry had recently purchased to train for racing.

Kaden had reached out to him, projecting feelings of peace and joy, just as he had been practicing with other, domesticated animals. The horse was different, however. Instead of being filled with fear and trepidation, it was filled with anger and restlessness. Kaden perched himself against the gate fencing the stallion in and lost himself in his concentration of sending his feelings to the massive, quivering creature.

The stallion had continued to prance about the large enclosure, wary of his presence. After endless minutes passed, he had opened his eyes to the large head of the horse butting him on the shoulder. Suddenly, the emotions of the stallion were flung back at him, enveloping him in a shroud of anticipation, curiosity and warmth.

It had been the most thrilling moment of Kaden's life. Feeling another creature as eager to accept him as he was to accept it. Before long, he'd crawled under the gate to join the horse and they had chased each other around the paddock until Kaden had become too tired to continue.

He almost fainted from expending energy he didn't have due to lack of food, but it had been well worth it. Only when the stallion had reared back and run full speed to the other side of the paddock had Kaden noticed the tall man approaching the fence. He'd been about to imitate the actions of the horse and bolt, when he'd heard the first kind words out of Henry's mouth.

"Son, you must have some shiny, brass balls between those scrawny legs of yours. I ain't never seen a man gentle a wild stallion the way you just did Lightning here. I'm in need of a horse whisperer with your talent. The job's yours if you want."

Since then, Kaden had been able to use his gift in a way that gave him freedom and happiness like nothing else ever had in his life.

The money and generosity Henry had bestowed upon him had allowed him to collect his sister from the old friend of his mom's and bring her out to live on the ranch with him. It was like a dream come true. But it was also one he was constantly putting in jeopardy with the attention he drew, no matter how much he tried to make himself invisible.

Kaden saddled up Mockingbird and took her through her paces, then turned his attention to the other horses he was preparing for a show they were scheduled to perform for in a month's time. The day was long, and Kaden wasn't able to end it until several hours after sundown, but he was satisfied with his progress and felt safer than he could remember feeling in a long time.

The farm-hand that had stood up first at the breakfast table that morning and punched Jim in the nose had come to him at midday to talk. Kaden had shied away at first, but the man had seemed to sense his wariness and stayed a respectful distance away.

Kaden tried desperately to remember his name— *Tam? Tim?* —before the man spoke, saying, "I don't exactly know what went on between you and that asshole yesterday, and I didn't come here expecting to find out. A man's business is his own. But I want you to know that you can come to me if anyone gives you any more trouble. Me and the boys here have seen the miracles you work with these horses, and we're not inclined to lose you."

Kaden, who had always avoided the company of the men he worked around, had stood there in shock, not knowing how to treat this gesture of goodwill. The man— *Tim, yes that was it* —had simply tipped his hat and walked on as if he offered that kind of sentiment on a daily basis.

Well after dark, Kaden entered the main house through the back door of the kitchen and grabbed an apple before retreating to the small side apartment he shared with Missy. After finding her fast asleep in her bed, and giving her a light kiss on the cheek, he showered and scrubbed off the layer of dirt and sweat from the day's hard labour.

Donning a pair of long johns, he crept soundlessly to the living room and opened the window before arranging his blanket on the couch he used as a bed. The bungalow only had a single bedroom, and once he'd brought his sister down, there had been no question as to who would occupy that room. A teenage girl needed her privacy.

He lay there awake, as was his habit, and enjoyed the night's cool breeze as it wafted over his bare chest, and tried to empty his mind of the painful memories that always plagued him in the silence.

Chapter Two

Kaden had just started to doze off when he heard odd sounds drifting in through the open window in the living room. He glanced sleepily at the alarm clock on the end table and saw that it was past two in the morning. He contemplated going back to sleep as the noise persisted, but his curiosity got the better of him.

The ranch was usually quiet except for the sounds of insects from midnight to five in the morning, when everyone started to wake for the day. So the fact that he was hearing sounds at this time of the night told him that something was definitely wrong. Kaden knew that if it was an intruder, he wouldn't be able to stop him, but he could at least find out what was going on and report it to Henry if need be.

He changed into a pair of work jeans and a black shirt, leaving his boots off to better traverse the outside area in silence, then slipped out of the house and down the path leading to the barn. The entrance to the building was about thirty yards away and he paused to make sure that the noises were coming from that direction.

He heard what sounded like fierce growls coming from inside and instantly started heading that way, fearing that a pack of wild dogs might have gained entrance and were trying to get at the horses stabled within. He crept up to the sliding doors and noticed that they were cracked open slightly, which meant that someone had to have opened them from the outside.

As he squeezed his slender body through the crack and slid immediately to the side of the doors to remain unnoticed, the sounds of fighting and growling grew louder and Kaden was struck by the familiarity of them. He'd heard sounds like these before and, for a moment, he was rendered immobile by memories of the past. They swept through him like a tidal wave, threatening to steal his sanity, but he managed to tamp them down before they could consume him.

A sharp, piercing wail broke through the noise of the scuffle, propelling Kaden forward. He knew he should run and wake Henry to alert him to the possibility of danger. But, again, curiosity won out and he felt compelled to inch his way forward, staying hidden in the shadows provided by the stall walls.

By this time, the horses had begun to react to the violence occurring so near to them. Kaden tried to reach out and project feelings of calmness, but their minds were in a haze, too confused to heed his attempts to bring them peace. When he finally reached the last barrier between him and the figures, the fighting had begun to slow and the growls had lessened in volume.

A sense of dread settled in the pit of Kaden's stomach and the urge to run as far and as fast as possible was almost too much to deny. But he forced himself to peek his head out from around the wall he was hiding behind and sucked in a disbelieving breath at the sight before him.

Terror gripped his entire being as, one by one, the wolves turned at the noise of his sharp intake of breath and stared at him with eyes that glowed in the moonlight. That's when their scents hit him. All rational thought left his mind as their identities became clear to him, just as he was sure his own identity was recognised by them.

The blood that coated their muzzles, the disembowelled body that now lay lifeless upon the hard-packed earthen floor, the tone of their growls, which had gone from menacing to excited upon sight of him—none of this bothered him. He'd seen it all countless times with these very wolves in the past. What had his heart trying to beat its way out of his chest was the fact that they had found him.

Kaden wanted to scream, cry, shout at them to go away, but he could do none of those things. They had found him, and they would take him back to their Alpha. The thought of the punishment he would receive for running caused a small groan to escape his lips.

The largest wolf, in the middle, whom he knew to be Thomas, shifted to his human form, confirming Kaden's suspicions. He stalked towards Kaden slowly, as if he had all the time in the world after committing murder. Kaden felt his gaze lower to the man's waist and his body cower before him, assuming the position of submission that had been beaten into him for years.

"So this is where you've been hiding, little half-breed. Alpha Gregory will be so pleased to have you back again. In fact—" he spared a glance for the wolves flanking either side of him—"I think we should remind you of your duties before we take you back. Gregory always was selfish when it came to you."

Kaden could feel the acid from his stomach burning its way up to his throat and his body start to shake uncontrollably as Thomas lunged at him, bringing the back of his hand across Kaden's face. Blood burst from his lower lip and nose but he barely felt the blow before his body was tackled to the ground. The oppressive weight of the man on top of him crushed him into the hay and dirt on the floor.

Suddenly, one of the wolves let out a low warning growl, which pulled Thomas's attention away from Kaden and had him sniffing the air to determine the threat that the other wolf had sensed. Kaden's head was still reeling from the strike dealt to him, but he managed to open his eyes just in time to see Thomas shift back to his wolf form and herd the others out through the front entrance.

They retreated in a haste that left Kaden confused and more than a little scared as to what could possibly have caused them to run away. Blood was pooling in his mouth and he turned to spit it out but couldn't get his limbs back under control enough to rise.

Fear was still coursing through his body unchecked a few minutes later when he heard another sound. Thinking the trio had eliminated whatever threat they had perceived and come back for him, he curled into a ball, knowing that he stood no chance against their superior weight and strength.

Kaden desperately tried to keep himself from hyperventilating as the sound of paws padding along the earthen floor drew closer. It was the scent of the wolf that reached him first, well before he could make out its form in the dark interior of the barn. The smell of musk, evergreens, and the cloying aroma of rich, damp earth hit his nostrils and recognition slammed into him with a force that made him gasp.

It's him! Michael. The one were he'd never thought to see again in his life. The one who had rejected him so many years ago was stalking towards him in a slow, purposeful gait. The wolf crossed the distance between them in one leap, shifting swiftly to his human form so that when he landed, he was hovering above Kaden on his hands and knees.

The man, suddenly larger than life, reached down to gently lift Kaden's chin. So much emotion came through in that simple, warm touch. Joy, fear, desperation—but it was the overflow of excitement that, when combined with his own, made his entire body vibrate uncontrollably.

Michael tilted Kaden's face to the side and a wave of anger rolled through Kaden. He knew the man had noticed the dark splotching on his face that could only be bruises and blood. Kaden watched the face above him contort in rage. Suddenly, his shirt was torn apart down the front, followed hastily by his pants, until his pale skin was unveiled to soak up the soft beams of moonlight shining through the slats of the rafters above them.

The man swept his hands almost reverently over Kaden's exposed skin, searching for signs of further abuse. The only thing that kept Kaden from fighting back was the constant skin-to-skin contact and the emotions still pouring into him, letting him know that the larger man's anger was not for him.

"Mine!"

Kaden felt a ripple of electricity spear through his body at the depth of emotion in that one word. His paralysing fear turned to jittery anticipation as the massive form of the man who had walked away from him loomed over his now-naked body.

He tried to remember all of the reasons why he despised Michael. The hatred he'd nursed for him over time had been a means to help him cope with all of the pain and degradation he had been forced to withstand. But his mind wouldn't cooperate.

All he could recall was the shameful secret he'd never been able to admit to anyone. Not even to himself in the light of day.

He wanted this. Had been privately harbouring the hope that one day, this powerful stranger would come to rescue him, claim him. But it was too late now. He'd been forced to fight for his survival alone, and he'd been okay with that.

So why was his heart hammering in his chest and his body humming with exhilaration?

The feel of the man's hands upon his body were like trails of fire seeping just beneath his skin and burning him from the inside out. When Michael leant down and pressed his full lips to Kaden's, he moaned into his mouth. To Kaden's utter mortification, his body began writhing in complete abandon against the mass of muscle and flesh above him.

His conflicting emotions were almost overpowered by the stranger's more intense feelings of need and lust. He was belatedly surprised that they didn't cause him the sensations of pain or nausea he'd grown accustomed to when someone projected their emotions of desire and hunger into him through touch.

Kaden was shocked by the intense feeling of Michael's cock rubbing forcefully against his own. He gasped and arched his back, grinding into him with such passion that he thought he would burst at any second.

Shaking his head, he tore his lips away, gasping for air. Kaden tried in vain to remember why getting himself involved in any way with this man was anathema, but for the life of him, he couldn't get his brain to function properly. Strong hands were everywhere, grasping and pinching and massaging until he felt that he might shatter from the pleasure of their touch.

"I'm sorry, little one," Michael whispered against his neck in such a pleading tone that Kaden could not doubt his sincerity. "I must have you. Please!" The gut-wrenching, heartfelt plea from such a large, commanding man was Kaden's undoing.

A niggling, faint voice at the back of his mind screamed at him to stop this — to end this whirlwind of passion that was threatening to rob him of his very independence. But he knew he was just as much a prisoner of this violent arousal as the dominating man that held him so close.

"Yes," he whispered. "Please, yes!" No sooner had the words left his mouth than he felt the hard length of a huge cock pressing against his tight hole. Kaden tensed, bracing himself for the pain he knew would come from taking a cock into himself dry, but at the last second, the man spat into his hand and lowered it to lubricate his jutting member as much as possible.

The gesture reached into Kaden's heart and created a small fissure in the wall he had so painstakingly built around it.

"I'm sorry. I can't wait any longer. Forgive me," the stranger said as he thrust his cock deep inside. They both yelled out, and though he could feel the burst of pleasure that bowled into him from the other man, his scream was one of pain.

He squeezed his eyes shut, trying to breathe through it, but was immediately struck by such a strong current of shame that he opened them again. The sight of tears pricking the eyes of the strong man above him caused the sliver in his heart's encasement to widen. The stranger kept his body still for several seconds, licking along Kaden's lips, his jaw, and the hollows of his throat, giving him the time he needed to adjust to the sudden invasion.

"Please forgive me. Please." Slowly, Michael pulled back his hips until the head of his cock almost burst free of its confinement, then shoved it back in with a force that he seemed incapable of stopping.

Kaden quickly felt the initial shock of pain dissipate and surrendered to a pleasure so profound that he could do nothing but hold on to the man's massive shoulders as he was impaled over and over again by the largest cock he had ever taken into his body. It rammed into him with such force that if it weren't for the tight grip of the man's large hands on his hips, he was sure he would have slid head-first into the wall behind him.

Every thrust of that thick member grazed against something inside him that he had never known existed. It felt as though his body was about to fly apart, and yet the man's firm hold kept him grounded and gave him a sense of security he'd never experienced. Deep, hazel eyes caught and held his and the emotions he saw in them rivalled the ones that threatened to devour him in their intensity.

Warm lips pressed down against his in a desperation that stole his breath away. There was a startling jolt as the salty taste of the man's tears burst across his tongue, and he felt a tingling sensation race through his body. It started at his scalp and the tips of his toes and ran like rapid ropes of fire to his groin, where every feeling in his body coalesced into a burst that had him screaming out his release. At the same time he felt those lips leave his and a set of sharp teeth pierce the tender skin between his neck and shoulder.

Pain shot through him but quickly combined with the ecstasy of his orgasm, filling him with a magnitude of pleasure that was so ferocious and tender at the same time that his vision went black.

After two more powerful thrusts, a low growl rumbled against his skin and he felt warmth spilling into him, filling him. All he could hear was the pounding of his heart matching the fast-paced rhythm of the one beating through the chest pressed tightly against his.

Strong pulls of the mouth still attached to his throat brought on a multitude of vibrating and intense aftershocks that coursed through his system and refused to release him from his rapture. Eventually, the sucking slowed and came to a stop, much to his surprised chagrin, and he felt a rough tongue graze over the puncture marks on his neck.

For countless minutes, Michael lay there, encircled in the younger man's arms, trying to breathe through the shock of what had just happened.

He'd been tracking Stephen's scent for miles, to this large barn on a fairly vast stretch of land, but the smell that had hit his nose upon entering the building had taken over his senses. It'd invaded every part of his being until he was drunk with the fragrance of wild flowers and the tang of salty ocean spray.

His wolf's body had practically buzzed with the excitement of finding his mate and he had wanted to howl in exultation at the thrill of feeling complete again. For so long, he'd been living with an ever-widening pit of despair tearing his chest apart. To feel it heal itself within a matter of moments, all due to the simple presence of the tiny form beneath him, had been too much to hold in.

This man was his, and he would never allow him to disappear again.

Before he could find his voice to express his thoughts, though, a streak of fury speared through his body like a knife and the delicate arms of his mate fell away. The feeling disappeared once he raised himself up and lost physical contact, but that only left him feeling bereft and empty.

He stared down into the violet eyes of the young man beneath him, now narrowed in anger, and felt remorse tug at his heart.

The man raised his hands and shoved them at Michael's chest, delivering a blow of anger that was so strong, it sent him reeling onto his backside a good two feet away. The pain from hitting the ground was nothing compared to that which showed on the beautiful face before him.

With careful movements, Michael edged back towards the small figure of his mate when he saw him start to fold in upon himself with an expression that spoke of severe emotional pain. He placed a gentle hand on his mate's shoulder, wanting to regain that brief connection they seemed to have built during their torrid sexual encounter of moments ago.

Pain and anger and guilt slammed into him with just as much force as before, but this time he was prepared for it. A grunt escaped his lips as the feelings raged through him, but he was able to tamp them down, channel and redirect them to a separate part of his mind. The sudden understanding that the alien emotions coursing through him were his mate's feelings and not his own brought on a realisation that had him reeling.

"Oh shit, you're a mage."

Immediately after saying those callous words, he wished he could take them back, but the smaller man lying before him didn't seem to acknowledge his voice at all. Concern began to take the forefront of his emotions, which he was still trying to disentangle from those of his mate, when a faint whimper broke through his concentration.

"Please," a faint voice pleaded. Michael leaned in closer to his mate.

"What is it, sweetheart? What's wrong?"

The man tilted his head to the side and opened his eyes, allowing Michael to see all of the pain shining through them, pain that he could also feel just from touching him. The man reached out a trembling hand to Michael's chest and shook his head, pleading with his eyes and obviously trying to tell him something. It took him a few seconds before clarity dawned and he asked, "You can feel my emotions too, can't you?"

His mate gave a slight nod and Michael almost pulled back his hand before stopping himself. He knew all mages were gifted with some kind of ability. Although Michael still had a lot of questions about how the young man's particular gift worked, they would eventually need to get used to each other. Sooner rather than later.

His mate's eyelids drooped as if they had become too heavy to keep open.

Michael glanced at Stephen's ravaged body but didn't bother to check his vitals. Judging by the amount and temperature of the blood pooling underneath his body, Michael knew he was dead and had been killed not too long ago.

He was picking up three distinct scents apart from his mate's, but they were new to him, which meant that the killers belonged to another clan. The probability that his mate had been there during the murder had his heart racing with fear.

What might have happened had I not shown up in time?

It was too stressful to contemplate at the moment, and there was still work to do. He concentrated on the unique mental path he shared with all of his Betas and reached out to Dennis. The man had insisted on following him in a vehicle some distance away, just in case Stephen was unable to travel in wolf form when they found him.

"Dennis, I need a pickup down the road leading to Henry Connel's farm. I'm heading towards you now from his barn. Joseph, Nick, you're on clean-up duty. Stephen was attacked by at least three unidentified wolves that left before I got here. He's dead, so I'll need you to dispose of his body. Let's all meet up at my place once you're done here."

"Shit," Nick sent. *"Guess he finally got in over his head this time. Any clue as to which clan his attackers belong to?"*

"No, but I might have a possible witness."

"What are you going to do with this witness?" Joseph asked.

"Take him back to my place. I'll explain everything when we reconvene there."

There was a pause before they sent him their mental equivalents of assent and closed their link. Michael knew they had more questions for him, but those could wait until he had his mate safe and secure in his house.

He grimaced as he noted the damage he'd done to the smaller man's clothes in his haste to get at his body. It would only take Dennis about ten minutes to meet them, and he needed to find something to wrap him in. Aside from the chill in the air, there was no way he would allow anyone else to see his mate naked.

Looking around the barn's interior, he spotted a shelf with a few rough, cotton blankets and supposed that would have to do.

"I'll be right back, okay?"

His mate remained unresponsive, which was starting to worry Michael, but there was nothing he could do at the moment. If the man was simply in shock, that would be the least of Michael's worries. He crossed to the other side of the barn and grabbed one of the blankets from the shelf, keeping his eye on his mate the entire time. He shook out as much dust and hair as he could and draped it over the other's crouched body, then scooped him up into his arms.

He caught a glimpse of the lost look on his mate's face before it was pressed against his chest—in an effort to hide from him, no doubt. As Michael slipped through the sliding doors of the barn and began to jog around the main house to the road beyond it, he tried to focus on his emotions.

His mate had acknowledged that he could pick up on Michael's feelings when they were touching, just as Michael could pick up on his, so he pushed aside all of the turmoil and excitement of the night and concentrated on emanating warmth and confidence. It was a lot easier said than done, but after a few minutes, he felt the slight frame in his arms begin to lose some of its tension. By the time Dennis met them at the side of the road, the younger man was fast asleep.

Michael placed him in the back seat, then dressed in the spare set of clothes Dennis kept in his trunk. He climbed into the back and pulled his mate back into his arms, making sure that the blanket covered as much skin as possible as he caught Dennis staring at them in confusion.

"I'll explain it all as soon as everyone gets back to my place. Meanwhile, I need to get this pup into a warm bed. I think he might have gone into shock but he's sleeping for now."

Dennis nodded his head and didn't waste any more time getting them back to Michael's house. It took them almost twice as long to get home as it had taken him to reach Henry Connel's farm. There were no roads that cut straight through the countryside, which was one of the many benefits of travelling in wolf form.

For the entire trip, Michael worked to keep his emotions at bay, getting better at focussing on feelings of peace and contentment, but it was a struggle to maintain. The extreme joy he felt at finally having found his mate was tempered by the knowledge that he had claimed him almost against his will.

The smell of his mate's blood, combined with his mere presence after so many years of abstinence and longing, had robbed Michael of his better judgement. He'd very nearly lost all control, forgoing pleasantries and foreplay in his eagerness to possess him. Even though he knew the man had been aroused, that didn't justify his actions.

He only hoped that his mate could eventually forgive him. For everything.

As Dennis pulled into his driveway, he saw his father's pickup next to his own and assumed that Nick had related the news of Stephen's death to him. Even though Michael had taken over as Alpha of their clan four years ago after his father had retired, Sam still showed his support and gave advice whenever he thought it was needed.

Dennis parked the car as close as he could get it to the front steps, then jumped out and opened his door for him. Rising gingerly from the backseat, he settled his mate more comfortably in his arms and absently noticed his weight. The little guy couldn't be more than maybe one hundred and twenty-five pounds soaking wet.

Michael's protective instincts screamed at him and he was already planning out what he would make his mate for breakfast when he walked through the front door that Dennis held open for him. Once inside, he noticed that his father, Nick and Joseph had stopped talking to wait for him to join them in the living room, but he had to take care of his mate first.

He went straight to the couch, which Joseph was lounging on with his feet propped up on the coffee table, and growled down at the man. Joseph's eyes widened and he quickly stood up and moved out of the way as Michael proceeded to lay his mate down gently, making sure to keep his small body covered by the blanket.

He knew he should probably put the pup in his bedroom, or at the very least get him some clothes or a clean blanket, but he had things to discuss and he was reluctant to let his mate out of his sight for more than a few seconds. The enormity of finally finding him after years of painful and disappointing searching was still hard to grasp.

Michael knelt down beside the couch and leaned over his mate, tilting his head to the side to get a better look at the bruises on his face. They were healing already, but one looked older than the other, maybe by a day or two, letting him know that the other man had been injured on two separate occasions.

Had someone on the ranch been abusing him? Michael knew Henry personally. He'd given the older man financial advice on more than a few business deals over the years. There had been nothing in his character that caused Michael to think he would stand for abuse in any form, but his integrity didn't exactly extend to all of his employees.

A cough brought him out of his reverie, and he looked over to see his Betas staring at him with more than a little consternation. His father, however, was wearing a grin so wide that it was a miracle it didn't split his face in half.

Michael felt heat flush his cheeks as he pivoted his body to sit on the couch next to his mate, pulling the man's head into his lap.

"Is this the witness you were telling us about?" Nick asked. After Michael nodded, Nick followed with, "Do you know him?"

Michael hesitated at that question, but he couldn't bring himself to lie. They'd smell it on him anyway.

Taking a deep breath, he said, "Actually, we both know him. We first met him outside of that club you dragged me to four years ago." Michael watched as Nick took a step towards his mate and peered closer at his face. He knew the moment his friend recognised who his mate was because his expression changed from one of confusion to one of utter disbelief in less than a second.

"The…the whore?" Nick sputtered. Michael was on his feet and over the coffee table before he knew what he was doing, eyes locked on his friend's throat, but his father was even faster. Sam swiftly stepped in between the two men and took the brunt of Michael's forward momentum. Nick wisely backed up several steps while Sam struggled to keep his son in check. Once Michael had stopped snarling and trying to fight his way to his Beta, Sam released him but stood his ground.

"Son, I understand what you're feeling right now, but I think it's time for you to come clean."

Michael slowly let the rage bleed from his body and took in the compassion lining his father's face. It was time to tell the truth, and surprisingly, the words flowed from his mouth with a lot more ease than he had anticipated over the years. He'd spent so much time lamenting the loss of his mate that finally admitting that his mate was male and that he'd deserted him held no fear for Michael.

"This is my mate. I've known he was mine since he first approached me in the parking lot of that club so long ago. I..." Michael had to pause and swallow the surge of self-loathing that threatened to overwhelm him. "I rejected him because I thought that being Alpha of our clan meant that I should mate with a female. I denied him because he was male, and weak. And because I was worried about what everyone might think."

As much of a relief as it felt to finally confess his greatest mistake to one of the men he trusted most in his life, each excuse that he brought to light for abandoning his mate felt like a sharp knife through his heart.

"Wait, wait. Are you telling me that you let this pup roam around the streets for years, unprotected, because you were too chicken-shit to admit that he was your mate?" Nick exclaimed.

The sudden change of sides caught him by surprise, and this time, it was Nick that Sam had to stop with his body. Nick pushed himself away from Sam's restraining grasp and glared at his best friend in contempt. "Just tell me that you didn't wait this long to try to find him."

"Hell, no! I realised my mistake almost immediately. Why do you think I had you drive back to the club that night? But he was already gone. I let him down. I know that, and I will spend the rest of my life trying to make it up to him. I don't know..."

A small groan from behind him interrupted his defence, and he whipped around to see his mate stirring on the couch. Instantly, he rushed over to the slight form, concerned that the high emotions in the room might have affected him. He had no idea of the scope of his little mage's power.

The pup fluttered his eyelids before opening them, giving Michael a full view of that gorgeous, deep blue colouring. Those eyes, framed by thick, blond lashes, began to widen as recognition seeped in. "You," he whispered.

Michael tried to smile to allay some of the fears he knew must still be plaguing the boy, but it probably came out as more of a grimace. "I'm sorry, sweetheart. I didn't mean to disturb you."

Rage suddenly contorted the face of his mate and the man flung the blanket off his body before Michael could react and jumped over the back of the couch, out of reach. His naked form was bared for all to see, but Michael didn't think that's what held their attention so much as the scars that were now clearly visible under the bright lights in his living room.

His chest was covered in a latticework of thin, horizontal scars, both pink and silver, that stood out in stark relief against his pale complexion. From the brief glimpse of the man's backside, which he was sure his father and Betas had also seen, he knew that the scars covering his chest were nothing compared to those that decorated his back and ass.

"Oh, sweet Mother..." Sam breathed.

His mate's entire body vibrated, though whether it was from fear or anger, Michael couldn't tell. He suspected both. Once he managed to get over the initial shock of seeing the marks upon his mate's body, he picked up the discarded blanket and slowly walked around the couch to him.

"Let me put this back on..."

"*Don't.* Touch. Me," the man seethed.

Michael's assessment of his mate's mood was definitely veering towards anger. He continued to advance and tried not to let his surprise show when he saw that the man was standing his ground.

"I won't touch you. That causes you pain, doesn't it?"

The frightened man flicked his nervous gaze away from Michael for a brief second to take in the still forms of Michael's father and Betas. When his eyes returned to Michael, they were so full of pain and confusion that Michael felt his breath hitch in his throat.

"You left me. You left me and he knew."

"Who knew, baby?"

His mate swallowed convulsively and looked down at his body, as if just realising that he was naked. The salty scent of tears filled the room and Michael watched a few droplets fall to the floor as the young man tried to cover his groin as much as possible.

"It doesn't matter. I was ugly when I met you. He's made me hideous." The despair in the man's eyes as he raised his head and looked straight at Michael was more than he could take.

Michael threw the blanket down and dropped all pretence of subtlety, striding forward to take the smaller man in his arms, but a raised hand stilled his advance.

"You're looking for the murderers of the were that was killed earlier, aren't you?"

Michael was baffled by the sudden change in subject, but stayed where he was. He could tell that his mate was hanging on to his control by a thread, so he let him have it for now, not wanting to tip him past his breaking point.

"Yes. Did you see them?"

The man gave a bark of laughter that sounded a little hysterical, but his lips never curved into a smile. "I saw them. I know them. Very intimately."

That last part was said so quietly that none of them would have been able to make out his words if not for their superior hearing. Michael could feel an irrational bout of jealousy rip through his body and freeze his mind. He felt the growl rumble from his chest more than heard it and took an intimidating step forward but the sharp command of his father's voice pulled him up short.

"Son!"

"And what exactly was your relationship with them?" Michael knew the man had been turning tricks at the club. The possibility that his mate might have willingly given his body to men who were capable of cold-blooded murder had his body coiled in rage.

His mate seemed to forget about his nudity and clenched his fists by his sides, matching Michael's angry glare with one of his own. "You think I was fucking them? What do you care?"

The urge to claim his mate again took over. He needed to prove that the man was off-limits to all others. Without though, he launched himself at his mate, who tried to turn and run but it was far too late. He locked his hands onto thin upper arms and pushed him back against the wall at the same time Joseph grabbed him from behind, but he wouldn't release his hold on his mate. They all tumbled to the floor in a heap of arms and legs, but it was the young man's high-pitched, tortured scream that brought their struggle to a halt.

Chapter Three

Michael felt his jealousy and anger melt as the echoes of his mate's pained cry reverberated through his head. He shook off Joseph's hands and leaned over his now unconscious mate. His alarm reached new heights as he saw two thin trails of blood leak from his nostrils.

"Baby?" He checked the man's pulse, feeling no less anxious at finding it faint and erratic, and began to gently shake him. "Baby?" He choked back a sob and turned to look behind him. "Dad!" he shouted.

"Right here, son." His father's soft voice to his left calmed his frenzied thoughts a bit and he jerked his head around to stare into the man's eyes, taking comfort in the control he found there.

"I think he has mage blood in him. He told me he could feel my emotions when we were in the barn, and I could feel his also. I think I may have hurt him when I tackled him. I had so much anger in me.

Dad..." His voice broke at that moment but thankfully his father remained calm and held his desperate gaze.

"Do you trust me, son?"

The answer was immediate. "Of course I trust you, but..."

"Then let go of your mate and give him to me until you can get your emotions under control," his father said in a tone that was so matter-of-fact, Michael didn't hesitate to obey. He gently turned his mate's head into his father's waiting hands and sat back, taking deep breaths to try to regain his lost control.

All four men watched in amazement as Sam softly caressed the man's uninjured temple and quietly sang a song that Michael hadn't heard since his childhood when his mother used to sing him to sleep. His mate started to stir and snuggled his face deep into Sam's belly, curling his body towards Sam's lap like a child. After a few minutes, a round of startled gasps filled the room from everyone but his dad at the younger man's sudden laughter.

That's when it hit him.

A burst of joy so bright that it took his breath away swept through Michael, almost knocking him on his ass. He couldn't keep the bubble of laughter from erupting from his lips, breaking the thrall that had held him at watching his mate react so well to his father's soothing touch. Similar sounds echoed around him and he turned to see looks of awe and happiness on the faces of his Betas. They all broke out in stunned laughter, enjoying the simple thrill of being alive and in such good company.

After several seconds, the mood in the room began to change and they all became quiet but held onto that comforting glow of merriment. Michael looked back to see his father bent over the face of his mate, whispering something in his ear before looking up to meet his gaze.

"Son, you've got yourself a very fine mate, but he needs his rest. I want you to hold on to the joy you're feeling right now while you carry him up to your room. Mind, keep that joy in your heart at all times while you're touching him, hear me?"

Michael smiled and nodded, letting go of his fears and allowing his happiness to seep into every pore of his being before taking his mate from his father's lap. He held his precious cargo close as he climbed the winding staircase to his room. After toeing his bedroom door open, he stared in wonder at the beauty in his arms.

A slight smile remained on his mate's lips as he laid him down over the comforter and pulled the hand-crafted quilt his mother had made for him over his shoulders. He chuckled at the way the man curled into the quilt, and was absolutely stunned when his mate chuckled back, as if reading his thoughts. This was definitely going to take some getting used to.

He leant down to plant a chaste kiss upon his cheek before tiptoeing out of the room, leaving a slight crack between the door and the wall in case he woke before Michael could join him again. Michael returned to the living room and felt his smile begin to fade as he took in the disgruntled looks of his men. The mood in the room had decidedly taken a turn for the worse by the time he sat down on the couch and reviewed the events of the past few hours. Nothing made sense to him, and he found that the more he tried to put order to the chaos of the night, the more confusing it became.

Joseph was the first to break the silence by snarling out, "What the hell was that about?" They all shook their heads in agitation, feeling the same sentiment, until Michael caught the small, knowing grin on his father's face.

"Dad? Got something you'd like to share with us?" Michael asked.

Sam's grin broke out into a full-on smile at the question, but he quickly cleared his throat and attempted to school his expression into one of gravity, failing miserably. "I'm sorry, but can't a man take pride in the mate Mother Earth has given to his son?"

Michael furrowed his brow at that veiled response and continued to stare questioningly at his father. He knew that Sam had no qualms about his mate being male, but he hadn't expected this type of enthusiastic response, even if he'd introduced his mate under more favourable circumstances.

Sam cleared his throat again and finally adopted a more appropriate demeanour. "Son, you're right about him being part mage. I couldn't smell his power until I got close to him, but I suppose his were scent was masking most of it. All mages are born with a unique gift that can help their coven to prosper. They keep to themselves mostly. I've only met two in my lifetime, up in South Dakota and Michigan. A half-breed is almost unheard of. I'm assuming that since you found him working at a club, and then out at Mr Connel's ranch, that he is without coven or clan. Unfortunately, half-breeds are frowned upon by most weres and especially by mages."

He paused and took a breath as if to collect his thoughts. "Michael, do you realise the amount of responsibility that will come with claiming your mate, which I assume you've already done judging by the mark I saw on his neck?"

Michael felt his face flush and nodded, but his father only arched his brows at his non-verbal response. "I have claimed him, but I'm not sure what you mean by responsibility."

Sam dipped his head in acknowledgement before continuing. "It seems that your mate's power lies in being able to feel the emotions of anyone he's touching but, more than that, anyone who is touching him can project their emotions onto others through him. When I was—" Sam hesitated, searching for the right words. "—comforting my son-in-law, I was thinking about you and some of your more outrageous antics when you were growing up. The happiness I felt at those memories poured into him, then spread to all of you. Do you recall hearing him laugh before all of you joined in?"

Michael exchanged confused, yet slightly amused looks with the men around him.

"Wait, are you saying that...the happiness we felt...it came from you? The pup was sending your emotions into us?" Nick asked. "'Cause I gotta say, once I started laughing, I didn't want to stop. It felt good, but it was powerful. I don't think I would have been able to stop even if I had wanted to."

The enormity of his admission hit everyone and Sam took a moment to let that idea sink in.

"That's exactly what I'm saying." Sam looked each of his son's Betas in the eyes before turning back to Michael. "I think someone has already taken advantage of your mate's gift, given the scars on his body. It is now your responsibility to ensure that his gift isn't abused again."

"But what if the kid decides to use his gift against us?" Joseph asked. He looked at Michael and said, "No offence, man, but we still know next to nothing about him, and he's got a pretty damn effective tool that he can use—"

"No," Sam cut him off. "I don't think so. The only time any of you were affected by his gift is when I purposefully sent my feelings into the young man. Once he learns to use his power, he might be able to project his own emotions, but for now I think that he can only channel what other people send into him."

Joseph gave him a doubtful look, and Sam replied, "That pup was naked, in tears, and admitting his association with killers in front of a room full of men he had to know would kill him over that kind of confession alone. Yet none of you could pick up on his emotions then."

Nick, Joseph and Dennis all exchanged glances, knowing that Sam spoke the truth.

"But if that's so, then how is it I can feel his emotions when I touch him?" Michael countered.

Sam gave his son an indulgent smile and said, "He's your mate."

Three simple words, and yet they seemed to explain everything. Michael inhaled a deep, slow breath, trying to process all of the information his father had just thrown at him, but he couldn't think past his need to protect his mate at all costs. Sam had said the man's gift had most likely already been abused. And even if it hadn't, his mate certainly had. The countless scars on his body attested to that.

After taking another deep breath, he released it and directed his gaze to the others waiting on him.

Dennis, who had been unusually quiet throughout the whole ordeal, acted before Michael could speak. He strode forward and knelt down on one knee, holding out his hand to Michael, who took it in his firm grasp, and said, "Congratulations, Alpha Michael. I swear to treat your mate with all of the honour and respect I hold for you."

The sincerity behind those words shone out of the man's bright, sombre eyes. His gaze never wavered from Michael's as he recited the ritual blessings each clan member gave to his Alpha upon the recognised union with his mate.

Joseph and Nick were quick to follow his example, despite the reservations Michael could see in their eyes. He couldn't fault them for having their doubts. This wasn't exactly the most conventional coupling of an Alpha and his mate.

Their declarations made his chest swell with pride and gratitude, and he nodded to each in turn, even his father. As his men filed out of the house and sought out their vehicles to leave, Michael laid a staying hand on his father's shoulder before the man reached the front door.

"Dad, I was wondering if you could, well, if you and mom might..."

"Your mom's packing everything as we speak, and I do mean everything, with the exception of the kitchen sink. We'll take the downstairs guest bedroom across the hall from your office to give you guys some privacy upstairs. I figure about two weeks should give you both enough time to adjust?"

Michael let out a breath he hadn't realised he'd been holding and smiled gratefully at his father. He'd never met a mage before and had no idea how to handle his mate's power. The thought of hurting him again out of ignorance was more than he could bear. The support of his mom and dad living with them for a while to smooth over any emergencies that might arise, such as the one that had occurred earlier tonight, would be an immense help.

"Yeah. Two weeks should be perfect. Thanks, Dad."

Sam grunted and shook his head as he said, "Don't thank me yet. Your mother is so excited you finally found your mate that she's bringing over her sewing machine and measuring tape to size him up for an entire wardrobe. I feel sorry for the little guy already."

Michael laughed and replied, "Well, at least she's got good taste."

Sam spread his arms, showing off his well-muscled and lean figure, saying, "The best, son. We'll let ourselves in in about an hour. I've got the house-key. Go take care of your mate."

Michael chuckled and locked the door after his father left. Taking the stairs three at a time, he reached his bedroom in moments, but paused once inside to savour the beautiful sight of the young man lying curled over a pillow in the middle of his bed.

He looked almost the same as he had four years ago, only a little thinner, if that were possible. His platinum-blond hair fanned out around his head, creating the image of a halo, and the combination of his pale skin and delicate features made him seem so fragile.

Michael was beginning to think that was closer to the truth than anyone suspected.

He stripped off his clothes, tossing them into the hamper, then climbed onto the bed to stretch his considerably longer length alongside that of his mate.

Before touching him, however, Michael took several slow, deep breaths and mastered his thoughts and emotions, envisioning tranquillity.

This is definitely going to take some getting used to. But as he turned and pressed himself gently against the back of his mate, breathing in his unique, intoxicating scent of the ocean, he knew it would all be well worth it.

* * * *

Kaden awakened to the most wonderful sensation of being surrounded in warmth and strength. It seeped into his pores and invaded his being so completely that it felt as though he was wrapped in layers of steel clouds. He inhaled the scent of musk and a heavy forest after a spring rain and sighed.

That smell was captivating, exotic, and…familiar.

Where have I…? Realisation hit him a second before he snapped his eyes open to find two very large arms wrapped around his midsection. Memories of the previous night came flooding back and he could feel his body start to shake. He reached up with one hand to feel the raised ridges of teeth marks in the soft flesh between his shoulder and neck.

No. No no no no no, this is not happening.

"Good morning, beautiful," a deep, rumbling voice said from behind him. Kaden wanted to jump from the bed, or better yet, beat the man behind him to a bloody pulp, but a wave of sexual energy tore through his body with such force that he gasped.

His skin became so sensitive that he swore he could feel every hair on the body of the man pressed so tightly against his backside. He also became increasingly aware of the cock that was swelling in the crevice between his thighs. Even as his mind rebelled against his reaction, his arousal grew to a sharp, almost painful point.

Kaden tried to remember all of the reasons why he should hate the man who was causing his body to respond in a way that it never had for anyone else before. He tried desperately to find his anger, but when he felt a tender kiss against the nape of his neck at the same time that a hand reached around to grasp his aching cock, all of his thoughts scattered.

His hips began to move of their own accord, rocking into that firm grip that he silently prayed would never let go. He wanted more, needed more, but the arm still banded around his waist held him still, forcing him to endure the slow, languid strokes of that hand. He bit his lip in an effort to keep from begging Michael to increase his speed. Kaden refused to let him know how much he wanted this pleasure. More pleasure.

A soft chuckle vibrated through the chest pressed against his back, and he felt more than heard the man whisper into his ear, "Like that, do you?"

A moan escaped his lips before he could suppress it and he felt what little resistance he had tried to retain melt away under Michael's skilful hand.

"Turn over, boy. I want to see you."

Kaden obeyed the command without a second thought, rolling over to get caught in Michael's hazel gaze, shadowed by the fall of silken, black hair.

His features were remarkable, but the look of wonder and desire in those soft eyes almost had him coming beneath the blanket. He flicked his tongue out to moisten his suddenly dry lips and felt his breath catch as he watched the man dip his head down and felt him swipe his own tongue along them, groaning into him.

Michael shifted his body over so that his weight was braced on his forearms and he hovered over Kaden, delving his tongue inside as soon as Kaden parted his lips. The few inches of air that separated their bodies seemed like miles, but he wasn't ready to close that distance just yet. He felt as though he was being swept away by his own arousal, betrayed by the lust consuming his body.

The big man broke off their kiss and peered down into his eyes as though searching for something. "I don't want to rush you this time. If you want me to stop, I will. Just say the word and…"

Kaden felt an irrational bout of irritation that the guy would get him so worked up, so heated and desperate to find release, then back off as though his sexual ministrations weren't a form of torture all their own. He effectively cut off the frustrating words by raising his hips and grinding his erection against that of the gorgeous man.

They both let out low moans and, before Michael could recover, Kaden set a fast rhythm. He ground their cocks together, building so much heat between them that it felt like thousands of tiny electrical shocks were coursing through his body all at once.

He couldn't believe his wantonness and aggression. During the long nights of loneliness and pain spanning the past several years, he'd always dreamt of what making love would feel like. Though this didn't quite involve love, the passion that was blazing through his body was as close as he'd ever come.

"I need to know. Tell me you want this too."

The honesty in the emotions pouring into him tipped him over the edge. "Yes," he hissed.

Michael growled and leaned to the side, quickly pulling a bottle of lube from the drawer of the nightstand beside the bed and pouring some onto his fingers. "Lift your legs, boy."

Kaden immediately pulled his knees up to his chest and whimpered as he felt rough fingertips rimming his puckered, sensitive hole.

Even though he was trembling in anticipation, the two fingers that eased into him had him clenching the muscles in his ass and crying out. The slight burn he felt was quickly replaced by a jolt of pleasure so intense that it flushed through his entire body, leaving him quivering and in need of more.

Michael began to twist his fingers, scissoring them until he hit the same spot inside him that he'd felt last night. Each time the large fingers grazed over it, Kaden swore he saw stars.

"Wh—what are you doing?" he stammered. "What is th—that?" It was almost impossible to form coherent thoughts while experiencing such wonderful stimulation.

A third finger was inserted and the large man began pumping them in and out, hitting that sweet spot with each pass.

"Haven't you ever had someone play with your prostate while getting you ready?"

Kaden squeezed his eyes shut and shook his head vigorously. This was nothing like the sex he'd known.

Michael frowned at that response but didn't comment, instead asking, "Think you can take all of me now?"

"Yes. Yes, please...more." He was shocked by the pleading note in his voice. He had never begged for sex before, but then again, this was a vast improvement on the pain it usually entailed. The invading fingers were pulled away and Kaden watched as Michael coated his cock with a liberal amount of lube before taking it in hand to guide it towards his stretched hole.

Kaden tensed and felt a sliver of fear at the feel of it pressed against him, begging for entrance, but then there was the glorious touch of lips brushing along his oversensitive skin, kissing his brow, his cheeks, and the arch of his neck. Hands caressed his chest and sides, spreading their warmth in long, gentle sweeps that eased his anxiety almost immediately.

Slowly, inch by inch, the man slid his considerable length into Kaden's tight hole, causing ripples of pleasure to streak down his spine and override the brief pinch of entry.

"Relax and open yourself for me. I won't hurt you, I promise." Michael leant forward and took possession of his mouth in a searing kiss that scattered his thoughts and eventually melted his muscles. The tight grip his ass had on the large cock began to loosen, until the huge member finally slid in completely.

The other man bit down gently on his bottom lip and began tweaking his nipples between the fingers of one hand while using the other to gather up the pre-cum leaking from the tip of his cock and spread it to lubricate his rock-hard erection. Small gasps were pulled from his throat, swallowed greedily by an eager mouth.

"That's it, baby. Give yourself to me."

The cock was slowly withdrawn from his passage and, just as it skimmed over that hidden nub that sent shards of pleasure racing down his spine, Michael rammed himself back into Kaden's body. His hips soon began a fierce pounding that Kaden was powerless to stop.

The violent force of the man's thrusts had Kaden squeezing his eyes shut again and reeling at the intensity and thrill of the mounting pressure. He reached his arms up and braced his hands against the headboard, afraid he would lose himself if he let go. The large man began pumping Kaden's cock in time with his gruelling pace, placing his other hand on Kaden's shoulder to keep him still, but it wasn't necessary.

Kaden arched his body to meet each of his thrusts with one of his own, taking the massive cock so far into him, he thought he might never recover.

Suddenly, the building heat caused by the friction of their bodies coming together became too much to hold in and Kaden's whimpers turned to loud cries. He felt razor-sharp canines pierce his neck and the pressure coiling in his body burst in a torrent of ecstasy. His body convulsed with the force of his release, leaving him utterly at the mercy of the huge man still pummelling into him.

The growl that emanated from the mouth clamped onto his neck forced several aftershocks to ripple through him. Finally, there was one more deep thrust and Kaden felt himself being filled and revelled in the glow of bliss that suffused his body and mind. The man withdrew his teeth from his neck, gliding his tongue across the mark he left behind in a soothing caress, and rolled over onto his back, pulling Kaden with him until he was draped across his chest.

They lay there for several minutes afterwards, trying to catch their breath and slow the pounding of their hearts. Kaden felt hands trail lazily over his back, tickling his skin for countless minutes.

"What's your name? I can't keep calling you boy all of the time."

The question brought Kaden back to the reality of their strange relationship and he knew he should get up now. Leave. Fight. Argue. Anything to get away from this man. He had spent every day hating the guy for the better part of four years, but at the moment, he couldn't even bring himself to lift his head. It felt as if his muscles had melted into the immense frame beneath him.

The comfort and safety that suffused his being from the tender embrace warred with his sense of self-preservation. He contemplated giving the man one of his aliases, currently Jade, but changed his mind, knowing he would probably find out the truth eventually.

"Kaden," he whispered against the neck he had pressed his face into.

"My beautiful Kaden. I'm Michael." A few more moments passed before he asked, "How did you get these scars?"

Kaden felt his body tense as the physical reminders of what Michael's rejection had left him vulnerable to were brought to his attention by such a blunt enquiry. Humiliation swept through him and he started to pull away, but the arms encircling him only tightened, holding him in place.

"Wait, I'm sorry. That was a bad choice of words and shitty timing. You can tell me when you're ready, just...let me hold you for a little longer. I've spent so long without you. I don't want to let you go just yet."

Okay, bad choice of words again. He shoved himself up from Michael's chest and gave him an incredulous look.

"You never had me," Kaden seethed. "You rejected me the moment you saw me. What? Am I suddenly good enough for you now?" By this time, his whole body was trembling and he broke out of Michael's hold, stumbling to his feet beside the bed. "Because I was kept a slave for over two years after you met me, so you might want to rethink your words."

Tears of anger threatened to spill over his lashes but he blinked them back. He wasn't even aware of what he'd revealed until he saw Michael's eyes narrow on him.

In a low, cold voice, the man said, "Who kept you a slave?"

"What?"

"You said you were kept as a slave. Did someone force you to use your power, Kaden? Is that how you got your scars?"

Kaden couldn't handle remembering his past at that moment. Couldn't handle the memories Michael's questions brought to the surface, or the look of anger on the man's face, a look he had no right to wear. Michael had abandoned him. Left him to the mercy of a madman. He had no right to act the avenging protector when he had thrown that role away so many years ago, just as he had thrown Kaden away.

Kaden had to get out. Get away.

Now.

He span around and started opening the drawers in the dresser to his left, frantically looking for something he could wear so that he wouldn't have to run away naked this time.

Been there, done that.

He pulled out a long, black T-shirt and tugged it over his head, not bothering to find a pair of pants. They would only end up falling off his skinny hips anyway.

"Kaden! What are you doing?"

Years of learning to obey commanding tones like the one that came from Michael almost overrode his new-found courage, but he shook it off and headed for the door, his anxiety increasing by the second. The man moved so fast, he didn't have time to react before a strong hand made contact with his bare arm and waves of crushing, maddening anger tore through him until he felt his knees buckle and a scream was ripped from his chest.

Michael instantly let go, but the brutal pain still reverberated through him, the trauma forcing blood to trickle from his nose and down the back of his throat. Kaden lurched to his feet and flung the door open, staggering down the hall and heading for the staircase.

"Kaden, wait!" Michael yelled, but he wasn't paying attention.

It took all of his effort to focus his blurred vision on the stairs, trying to make sure he didn't topple over because of his lost equilibrium. Kaden heard nothing else until he reached the bottom of the stairs and, in a desperate burst of energy, he ran to the front door, struggling to unlock it with hands that shook too much to get a firm grasp on the knob.

"Kaden!" Michael yelled.

He had just succeeded in opening the door when Michael ran forward and slammed it closed again, thankfully making sure to avoid contact this time. Kaden span around and headed for a window, determined to escape through it if need be, but Michael was faster, cutting off his path with the mass of his body. He looked around frantically but there was nowhere left for him to run.

As soon as that realisation hit him, he backed himself against the nearest wall and crumpled to the floor, fear robbing his limbs of strength.

"Son?"

Kaden tried to block out their voices, not interested in the slightest in what they had to say. He just wanted to go home, hold his sister, and forget that any of this had ever happened. She must be so worried by now.

"Dad. Help him, please. I think I hurt him again. I touched him in anger but I...I never..."

When silence descended upon the room, Kaden peeked through the locks of hair hiding his face. He danced his gaze about the room, hoping that by some miracle he had missed another path of escape, but when he saw Sam take a few cautious steps towards him, he began to hyperventilate.

His mind was a maelstrom of terror. All he could think about was that he was being held against his will. Again. Fear that he would be forced to use his power to harm and manipulate people again while his body was used for pleasure was too much to bear. The memories of Gregory using him were bad enough, but the possibility that his mate—a man whom he still felt an attraction for despite his better judgement—might hold him captive for the same reasons had him close to hysterics.

Kaden began to shake his head violently from side to side, trying to force the volatile thoughts from his mind, when his gaze was caught by a graceful woman running into his view in a flurry of lace and printed flowers. Her auburn hair whipped behind a face that seemed so welcoming, it stilled his thoughts and movements.

She wore a bright yellow sundress with patterns of colourful flowers on it that flared out from her ankles in her haste. Her heart-shaped face glinted with kindness that was so at odds with the fear coursing through Kaden's body that he hadn't realised she was upon him until he felt the light touch of her hand on the side of his face.

The happiness and love she was feeling conflicted with his darker emotions and he struggled to maintain the distinction between his own and those of the woman touching him.

"My, you are a pretty one, aren't you? Or is it handsome? They mean the same thing to me but some of these macho types," she waved her hand around to encompass the two large men behind and to the side of her, "tend to get a little stuffy over what you call them."

Kaden didn't know whether to feel perplexed or offended by her odd behaviour, but the joy he could feel emanating from her was beginning to permeate his being. She absently twined her fingers through his and leant forward to whisper in his ear in a low, conspiratorial tone, "Don't let the big man behind me fool you. He may look scary, but he's really just a big softy. Did you know that when he was six, he had an imaginary friend he wanted to dress as for the Solstice celebration and it turned out to be Papa Smurf?"

Kaden turned his wide eyes to see a deep flush creeping up Michael's neck and into his cheeks.

The woman leaned closer still and whispered with a huge grin on her face, "I have pictures!"

"Mom!"

She burst into laughter that sounded like bells chiming and lit up her face like a breathtaking sunrise. Her spirit and happiness within seemed as bright as the sun, and it warmed Kaden like nothing else ever had. He felt an unaccustomed smile curve his lips and he tightened his fingers around hers, not wanting to give up this unexpected ray of sunshine.

She began to wipe away the blood that had stopped flowing from his nose with the hem of her dress, never skipping a beat.

"One summer when he was about, oh, thirteen I think, Michael had convinced himself that he could fly and took one of my best sheets to use as a parachute and jumped from a thirty-foot cliff into a lake. Well his father, Sam, the lumbering caveman over there," Kaden followed her gaze over to the other man, "had never told him about the wisdom of crossing his legs before hitting the water. He couldn't sit down after that for a week!"

Kaden cringed at the pain he imagined that must have caused, but the look of embarrassed helplessness Michael shot at his father had both Kaden and the woman laughing now. Her joy was absolutely infectious.

Kaden felt himself get caught up in her excitement as she helped him from the floor and wrapped an arm around his waist, steering him into the kitchen. "Oh! I have to tell you about the time he shaved his head and..."

"Mom!"

Chapter Four

Michael stared, dumbfounded, as his mother spirited his mate away, chattering on about the most humiliating moments of his life. Somehow, in the span of one hour, the morning had gone from blissful to volatile to cheery, and in that moment, Michael was absolutely certain that his mate would be the death of him. He looked to his father for support but the goofy grin on his face as he stared after his wife told him that he was on his own.

Sam caught his gaze and shrugged. "The woman has her evil ways, but she always gets the job done."

Michael had to grudgingly nod his head and sighed.

"So what was that all about?"

"I don't know. I asked him about his scars and he told me that..." He had to swallow his rage as he recalled the boy's words and the memory of the haunted look in his eyes. "Dad, I know he was just trying to survive by working in that club, but I think something awful happened after I rejected him. Dad, I think he may have been forced to…to…"

"Use his power?"

Michael closed his eyes and took a deep breath, reminding himself that as bad as it was for him to imagine that kind of past, his mate had been forced to actually live it. "And more."

Sam thought about that and slowly nodded his head. "Give him some time to adjust, son. Let your mother work her miracles while you work on controlling your emotions. That man's got a powerful gift, and until we know more about him, we need to take this one step at a time."

Michael took another deep breath, opened his eyes, and tried to concentrate on the positive side of the situation. He had finally found his mate again. The young man was within his protective care and his mother and father were completely accepting of the fact that he was male…and a mage.

Michael wouldn't necessarily define himself as gay, but there was no mistaking the desire he felt for his other half. Kaden was alive and safe and…was that country music coming from his kitchen? The voice of Reba McEntire suddenly filled the house and he followed his father into the kitchen.

The sight that met him took his breath away. Katherine had her arm entwined with Kaden's and the pair were literally twirling about as they gathered ingredients from the fridge and cupboards to make breakfast. His mom was swaying her hips, bumping them against Kaden's and singing along to the song, while Kaden laughed and did his best to keep up.

It was as if the disaster of just minutes ago had never happened and the man dancing and smiling before him was a completely different person. Kaden's responsiveness to the emotions of others was amazing, if a bit frightening.

He had never seen a more appealing sight in his kitchen before.

Michael sat down at the table with Sam and started to notice the care his mother was taking with his mate. She never once let go of him physically, managing to subtly keep in contact at all times. Holding his hand, touching his cheek, even hugging him occasionally. The sound of his mate's laughter was so light and innocent that it held him enthralled. For countless minutes, his world consisted of nothing but the joy that radiated from his mate as he helped Katherine cook.

When the food was done, his mom turned off the little radio he kept beside the refrigerator and handed Kaden a plate of bacon to put on the table. She had to relinquish her touch on him in order to carry the other dishes, and when Kaden turned around and spotted Michael sitting at the table, watching him, he faltered.

Michael wanted to reach out to him so that he would know his anger had passed, but didn't want to frighten him again. Instead, he pulled out the chair beside him then walked to the counter to pour everyone cups of coffee.

Once they were all seated, Katherine continued to keep the conversation light, talking about her plans for the day and asking about the businesses run by some of their clan members. As Alpha, it was his responsibility to keep their community prosperous and assist anyone seeking employment, loans, repairs, or anything else within his power to help with.

The duties far outweighed the pay, even though he did very well for himself, but he cared about each member of his clan and took pride in his work. They all tried to include Kaden in the conversation, but his only responses were monosyllabic and his shoulder-length platinum hair kept most of his features hidden.

Michael noticed that, by the time everyone else had finished eating, he had yet to take a bite of the food his mom had piled onto his plate. His mother rounded the table and leant down to place a kiss on the crown of Kaden's head. He flinched at the contact but sent a small smile up at her as she and his father excused themselves, retreating to the living room.

Michael remained seated and asked, "Not hungry?" The man just shrugged, so he added, "I really wish you'd eat something." After another shrug, Michael sighed. This was going to take a lot more finesse than he thought he had. "What were you doing out at Henry's ranch?"

Kaden finally lifted his head and gave Michael an indignant look. "I work there."

Michael tried not to show too much surprise as he asked, "Really? What do you do?"

"I'm a... I can pick up the emotions of animals and project mine into them. Henry hired me to train his horses."

"Wow. That's really great." Michael was extremely impressed by the man's ingenuity at finding a job which put his power to an excellent use. However, he imagined it also made Kaden extremely valuable to Henry, which might cause problems considering his mate would have to quit. After nearly four years of regret and loneliness, he knew he wouldn't be able to allow Kaden to commute to a job that would take him away from Michael for the better part of nearly every day of the week.

As if reading his mind, Kaden said, "I'm not staying here. I'll identify the killers and tell you where to find them, but I'm gone as soon as I can find some clothes. I'll reimburse you for any costs."

The thought of losing his mate again had his chest tightening to the point that he thought it might cave in on itself. "Kaden..." He had to choose his words carefully. He fleetingly considered pointing out the fact that the man would need to testify against the killers in front of a clan council, thereby forcing him to stay until that happened, but quickly tossed that idea. He wanted his mate to stay for the sake of their relationship, not because of an ugly obligation.

"Kaden, you're my mate. I don't expect you to forgive me for rejecting you the first time we met, but...I would like for you to give me a second chance."

Kaden began to shake and Michael could see all of his anger shining brightly in his deep blue eyes. "You don't deserve a second chance," he whispered vehemently. "He saw you turn around and leave. You, an Alpha. That could only mean that I was clanless, and he...he knew..." Kaden pressed his lips together so tightly they turned white before he bowed his head, once more hiding his face behind blond locks.

"Kaden, can I touch you? I know my words don't mean much to you. You have every right to be angry, but I want you to know what I'm feeling. How much I want to make up for my mistake. If you don't think my emotions are sincere, I'll drive you back to Henry's farm right now and give you some time. But if you do believe they are, give me at least a few weeks to show you how much I want this." He waved his hand to indicate both of them.

Kaden studied his face through his lashes and strands of hair and Michael found himself holding his breath, trying to give his mate as much time as he needed to think about his suggestion. It wasn't easy, and as the seconds dragged into endless minutes, he thought he would go mad from the suspense. Finally, Kaden took a deep breath and reached out his still-trembling hand to Michael and touched his forearm.

The man's emotions came through sluggishly at first. Michael could tell he was trying to hold them back. There was fear, uncertainty, confusion. All justifiable, but not what he wanted to invoke in his mate.

He reached inside himself and thought about all the nights he had spent longing for the small man he had been determined beyond anything else to find again and comfort the way he should have done so long ago. He recalled the joy he had instantly felt in the barn when his dream had come true. How he had finally felt whole once he'd completed the mating ritual, binding their souls together and allowing for the possibility of true happiness to grow.

Kaden gasped, looking straight at Michael, and he had no doubt that every emotion he was trying to emit to the man through touch was also shining from his eyes with just as much fervour.

After a deep, shuddering breath, Kaden whispered, "Okay. Two weeks."

The excitement and pleasure that bubbled up from Michael was sharp and overflowing, causing Kaden to snatch his hand back in surprise.

"I'm sorry. I'll work on that, but I am glad you decided to give this a chance. To give me a chance." Michael leant forward cautiously and placed a quick kiss on Kaden's lips. He felt an electric current pass between them and knew that the desire that suddenly coursed through him was not completely one-sided, but Kaden abruptly pushed his chair back and took his dishes to the sink.

"Sorry again. Can't seem to help myself. Wait!" Kaden paused just as he was about to empty the contents of his plate into the trash. Michael stalked over to him and glanced down at the dish. "You still haven't eaten anything."

The man sent him a confused look then shrugged. "Umm…I guess last night upset me more than I thought. I'll eat later."

Michael tightened his eyes, not believing him for a second, but decided to relent for now. While they both set about cleaning the kitchen, Michael said, "So I was thinking that we could head up to Grisham Lake today, take it easy. The weather should be nice."

"Don't you want to take my statement first? About the…the murder?"

"You said you knew the attackers, right? Do you think I should be worried about them disappearing?" Michael asked.

Kaden seemed to give that some thought, then answered, "No. I know exactly where you'll be able to find them."

"Good, then that can wait for a few days. Stephen's body has been taken care of and you deserve to take a break. So how about it?"

Kaden chewed his bottom lip and busied himself with wiping down the table and countertops. After everything was cleaned and put away and the young man still hadn't answered, Michael opened his mouth to suggest something else when he heard, "I don't have any clothes here."

"My mom already thought of that. She brought over some of my old clothes from my school-aged years that should fit you until we can get you some more. The woman's a pack rat."

"What about your work?" Kaden asked.

"I've spent four years searching for you and now I've only got two weeks to convince you to stay. I'm not wasting a single moment of it on anything but you." Michael could tell he was fishing for excuses, but he was confident in his ability to find a way around every single one of them.

Except maybe for whatever had just occurred to his mate.

Kaden jerked his head up and gave him a wide-eyed look that he was sure portended trouble. "Oh shit! I almost forgot about Missy."

* * * *

Gregory slammed the receiver down on the phone, cursing under his breath. Things were falling apart, had been falling apart since his little mage had managed to escape a year and a half ago. Without the kid's power, he couldn't manipulate the many investors, influential figureheads, and key members of his clan he'd been taking advantage of. They were starting to express their doubts and abandon deals with which he would have raked in a tidy profit.

Normally, he would have sent out search parties, but if word got out to his clan that he and his Betas had been hiding a half-breed among them, there would be a riot. It was unheard of, to say the least, and if they caught on to the fact that he'd been using the kid's power against them, he would be exiled.

A knock on his door disturbed his thoughts and he could smell Thomas on the other side. "Come." His Beta let himself in and sat down in one of the overstuffed chairs on the other side of his desk. Without looking up, Gregory said, "I just got off the phone with a snivelling mayor with more bullshit than backbone, so unless you have good news, I suggest you come back later when I'm in a better mood."

"Oh, I think you'll like this," Thomas replied.

Gregory finally met the other man's gaze and studied the pleased look on his face. Considering the fact that he and his Betas had been frustrated and on edge for more than the past year, that look could only mean one thing.

"You found him. Is he here?"

Thomas let out a grin and said, "I found him. I don't have him yet, but I will. Very soon. I just need to do some asking around first."

Gregory narrowed his eyes at the vague answer. "Thomas, I don't have time for your ambiguity. Spit it out and be quick."

Thomas wasn't affected by his foul mood. He'd been dealing with it ever since they were pups. Besides, the knowledge that he would soon be reaping the benefits of their former slave's power again felt too good to let anyone ruin it for him.

"We saw him in a barn on a farm just outside of West Plains, right after we finished killing that little cheat, Stephen. I would have grabbed him but we caught whiff of an Alpha headed our way and couldn't risk him seeing us near the body."

"Did the boy see you murder Stephen?"

"Maybe, but he's got blood on his own hands, and he knows we're close to finding him now. He won't tell anyone. He's not at the ranch anymore, so I'm assuming the Alpha took him back to his clan. There're only a few around that area, though, so it's just a matter of finding out which Alpha interrupted us that night. We'll get our little bitch back, sir."

Gregory could feel his excitement building but he managed to keep it from showing on his face. He wouldn't be satisfied until he had his slave locked in his bedroom where he belonged. "Good. I don't want you guys to come back until you have the boy in your custody, but you will keep me posted every day." Thomas nodded and jumped out of his chair, eager to get started on their search.

"Oh, and Thomas? If any of you touch him before you bring him to me, I'll cut your dicks off. He's mine," Gregory growled. He was going to have fun punishing his boy for leaving him. He watched his Beta swallow visibly then leave, before he let the slow smile of anticipation break out on his face.

* * * *

Kaden had grudgingly agreed it would be best to keep his whereabouts a secret from all those who didn't need to know — including Henry — until the murder investigation was resolved. Though he was certain he would lose his job, the alternative of Thomas finding him and dragging him back to Gregory was even less appealing.

Eventually, Michael had talked him into allowing Nick to pick up his sister and drive her back here to ensure her safety. Kaden didn't trust Nick and had voiced his opinion without hiding any of his contempt for the man, but he couldn't deny the sincerity of the man's intentions when he'd touched him to discern whether or not he was a threat to Missy.

After a brief phone call to Missy's cell phone, he had been confident that she would follow his instructions to pack a light bag and meet Nick half a mile down the road from the ranch. He hadn't been able to give her an explanation over the phone, nor had she asked for one.

Her level of trust in him was humbling and it had almost brought him to tears. He'd failed her and his mother so completely in the past that he knew he didn't deserve to have her in his life, but he was grateful all the same. The call had been placed nearly two hours ago, and he could feel his anxiety increasing with each passing minute.

Kaden cast a sideways glance at the huge man sitting beside him on the couch while they awaited the return of Nick with his sister. If he was honest with himself, he would admit that he'd been holding on to the fantasy that this gorgeous man would realise his mistake and come to rescue him ever since they'd met.

He'd dreamt that Michael would find him and take him away from his waking nightmare, show him that pain didn't have to exist every second of every day, but that was before Gregory had broken him. He knew the disgusting mass of scars that was his body — the ugly, broken spirit that was his, devoid of hope. He could offer this powerful man nothing but a used, empty shell.

And yet, there was still the desire for something more, something better…and he hated himself for it.

He would survive, though, like he always did. By the end of the two weeks, Michael would realise that he wasn't worth the trouble of keeping after all. He would come to his senses and find a mate that was worthy of his status, casting Kaden aside like the used-up goods that he was.

Again.

Until then, Kaden would keep his heart in the neglected box he had locked it in years ago and postpone his running.

Gregory's men had spotted him in Henry's barn, which meant that he couldn't return to working there without taking the risk of being captured by his tormentor again. He would need to run far and fast, and most likely have to do things to support Missy and himself that he didn't want to contemplate just yet. If he could stave off that necessity for even a few days, he would. His only regret in all of this was to have to force his fifteen-year-old sister to cut her roots and run with him.

At the sound of gravel scrunching underneath the tires of a car, he jumped up and ran to the door, not bothering to see if Michael or his parents were following, and flung it wide. Relief engulfed him as he saw the petite blonde bounce out of the passenger seat once the car came to a stop and race into his open arms, almost knocking him over.

"Jade! I'm so glad to see you. I was chatting with my friend Stacy about science this morning and she told me that her teacher told her that black holes were two-dimensional and I was like, ohmigod! Seriously? And so we went to the NASA.gov website and found out that they were four-dimensional and I was going to print out the page so she could take it to her..."

Kaden tried his best not to wince as her gaze finally turned to the people standing behind him at the bottom of the porch. Her eyes widened and a perfect O formed on her lips as she tried to slip past him to get a better view.

He gently pulled her back with an arm he wrapped around her waist and said, "Missy, these are some friends of mine. And you can call me Kaden here. It's okay." He turned to acknowledge them while still keeping hold of the girl. Pointing at the taller man with his other hand, he said, "This is Michael, and those are his parents, Katherine and Sam. We'll be staying as guests here for a bit, so try to remember your manners, okay?"

His sister studied all four of them—as Nick had gone to stand behind Michael—for a few moments before her face lit up as though an idea had suddenly struck her. *Please let it go, please let it go*, he begged silently, but his luck had never been that great, or even good, for that matter.

"Did you finally find a boyfriend? Which one is he? Wow, they're both so sexy. I'll bet it's that guy." She pointed at Michael. "Well, it's about damn time. I was beginning to think you were abstinent and not just gay. Not that I mind that or anything. Just gives me more time to keep you to myself, seeing as how you work all the time. Hi!" She reached forward before Kaden could stop her and extended her hand to Michael. "My name's Missy, short for Melissa. Did y'all meet up over at Henry's? I've never seen you around there before."

Kaden felt his stomach twist and fear renew itself as he raised his eyes to look at the man Missy was boldly shaking hands with. He'd forgotten to mention that Missy knew nothing of the years he'd spent out of her life, or the danger he was putting her in just by keeping her close.

It had taken him months after escaping to feel confident enough to take over the responsibility of caring for her, but in the end, there had been no choice, really. She was his salvation. His reason for living. He had no life without her in it.

He was absolutely stunned when Michael simply raised a single eyebrow at him and sent an indulgent smile Missy's way.

"We did. And you must be his sister."

Kaden suddenly regretted keeping her so sheltered when she practically melted at the man's deep, charming voice. Her cheeks flushed and she giggled, still grasping the much larger hand in her own delicate one.

"I am. Did Kaden ever tell you about the work I helped him with on his latest project with Mockingbird? I did all of the calculations for the area space and designed the layout. I would have done more but this ogre," she nudged a hip into Kaden's side, "said I had to focus on my studies more. As if My grades are..."

"Okay, Missy." Kaden stopped her before her tirade could reach full-blown proportions. Sam and Katherine let out soft chuckles as he said, "Manners, remember? Did you bring your laptop with you so that you could keep up with your homework?"

She rolled her eyes and retorted, "Of course. Like I thought you would give me a break while we're out here. I'm not that delusional. Oh, and don't forget you promised to buy me that encyclopaedia of plants online." She faced the group of onlookers and said, "That's my power. I love nature, and I can help plants grow, and…"

"Missy!" Kaden couldn't believe she'd blurted out that information in front of virtual strangers.

"What?" She cast him an innocent look. "They're weres, right? I can smell them." Missy quickly turned to Michael and Nick and said, "Not that that's a bad thing. You both smell really good. Kaden smells like sunshine, and I always tell him that he should stop working so much so he can provide the light for my flowers at home, but he just rolls his eyes and buys me another plant or makes me do my homework. Sometimes he can be a real pain in my…"

"Missy!"

She beamed him her most dazzling smile and gave him large, puppy-dog eyes while swinging her body from side to side. "But I still love him anyway. And you got hurt again. Yesterday it was just the bruise, but now your lip is busted. Was it that same asshole? Henry said he fired him, but I'll bust his…"

Kaden clamped his hand over her mouth and sent a weak smile at Michael, whose face had taken on a stoical expression. *Great.* He was going to have to invest in duct tape and Superglue for Missy for the remainder of their stay here. He ignored his sister's peeved glare and turned her in the direction of Michael's mom.

"See Katherine over there? I happen to know she's a much better cook than Cheryl Connel and she's got a whole box full of recipes she can share with you. If you promise to go back to your studies tomorrow, I'll let you take today off and experiment with her. Deal?"

Kaden didn't release her mouth until she was nodding her head in earnest, crossing her heart and bouncing as if her excitement would climb right out of her chest. As soon as he lifted his hand, she was back on track with her incessant chatter. "Can I help you? Really? Do you have a herb garden? I know all of them by smell."

Katherine burst out laughing and herded Missy into the house, showing the same wealth of patience with his sister that she had shown him. Sam gave him a nod before slapping Michael on the back and heading in after the women. Kaden was about to thank Nick for bringing Missy to him safely but hesitated when he noticed the man shuffling his feet nervously and hanging his head. He didn't need to touch him to know something was wrong.

Michael must have noticed it too, because he asked, "Nick? Was there a problem when you went to pick her up?"

Nick met their stares with raised eyebrows and shook his head while waving his hands in front of him. "No, no. It went fine. Kid's almost as sneaky as I was at her age. I don't think a single person there saw her leaving. I just..." Nick turned his full gaze on Kaden and spoke in a low voice. "I'm sorry. I misjudged you. Your sister's quite a talker...well, you probably know that more than anyone...but she told me how you've been taking care of her. She talked about nothing but you for an *hour* on the way over here."

Kaden felt a flush colour his cheeks and lowered his eyes to the ground.

"But she never lied, and she never had a bad thing to say. My Alpha is blessed to have a mate that loves and cares for his family that much. I apologise for not giving you the benefit of the doubt, either time we met." Nick extended a hand and held it a foot away from Kaden. "I'm hoping that you'll give me a second chance along with this undeserving dog as well." He jerked his head in Michael's direction, who actually managed to look offended.

Kaden glanced from one smirking yet sincere face to the other indignant yet proud one. He didn't quite understand what had just happened, but judging by the humour dancing in the eyes of each man in front of him, he figured it was a good thing.

A small smile tugged at his lips before he took Nick's extended hand and shook it. He felt all the emotions evident in the man's eyes, with no hint of deception, and decided to let go of the resentment he'd been harbouring for him.

* * * *

Their next three days together were spent in relative amiability among the company of his parents and his mate's sister. The girl had a mind as quick as her mouth, and an eagerness to use her gift of assisting anything that sprouted from the soil of Mother Earth that was nothing short of admirable. She contained a quality of exuberance that he could easily imagine had once thrived in Kaden.

Though the young man seemed to soak up the happiness of those around him, Michael was beginning to be able to detect the difference between his mate's genuine emotions and those of the people touching him, and he was saddened to find that it usually took another's happiness to ignite his own.

He had tried several times to speak with Kaden privately and, after the third thwarted attempt, had become noticeably frustrated. Fortunately, his father had intervened and it had only taken one look to remind Michael that his mate shouldn't be rushed.

His true test of endurance had come that first night when his man — *his mate* — had chosen to sleep with his sister in the other guest bedroom she had been given instead of with him. It had hurt. More than he would admit. Then Kaden had given him a soft, impulsive kiss goodnight without any influence from his end, and Michael had held on to the whisper of joy he'd felt leap from his mate to him for the rest of the night.

It occurred to him over the next few days that Kaden's reluctance to be alone with him was a test as well. He'd initially taken offence at the many guarded looks the man would send his way when he thought he wasn't looking, as though he was expecting Michael to pounce on him at any moment. Yet the more Michael kept his respectful distance, the more the smaller man seemed to initiate contact with him.

The nightly kisses grew heated, but always left him with nothing more than his hand for relief. It wasn't unlike trying to tame a wild, frightened animal, and he amazed even himself with a reserve of patience he'd never known he possessed.

On the fifth day, Kaden had demurely agreed to accompany him on a picnic.

Michael couldn't stop sending sideways glances over at the figure seated next to him during their drive to the lake. He was still trying to process the fact that he had found his mate after living for so long with the possibility that he had blown his only chance at a true mating.

The jeans and shirt his mom had brought over were from his years as a young teenager, but they were still big on the boy. He'd had to cut a hole in the shortest belt he owned to keep the pants from falling off his slender hips. The overall effect made Kaden look like a kid playing dress-up in his father's clothes, but there was nothing to do about it until they went to Henry's ranch to pick up his things.

Kaden had remained silent since their departure from the house and Michael itched to reach out and touch him, to try to pick up on his emotions, but thought it best to give the man his space for now. Michael couldn't always feel what Kaden was feeling when they touched. At some times his emotions were loud and clear and at others it felt as though they were just beyond shadows that he couldn't penetrate.

He wasn't sure if Kaden was consciously keeping them from him or not, but he still had time to work on it. When the lake finally came into view, Michael breathed a sigh of relief when he saw that there were very few people there. It was used for recreation and could get fairly busy during the tourist season, but it started growing quiet again towards fall.

He pulled his truck into one of the parking sites and turned off the engine. They both got out, and he grabbed a backpack full of food, water, towels and shorts they could change into in case they decided to take a swim. He walked up beside his mate and took in his look of wonder as he gazed out over the lake. The sun shone down on Kaden's hair, making it shine so brilliantly it appeared a shimmering white.

"Beautiful." Michael wasn't sure if he was talking about the delicate form beside him or the lake.

"Yeah," Kaden breathed. Rays of sunshine danced upon the lake that rippled from the slight breeze in the air and from the small clusters of ducks lazing about in the water. The leaves of the surrounding trees had turned several shades of yellow, red, brown and gold. Those that had fallen to the ground mixed their colours with those of the flowers that grew wildly across the acres of green grass.

Michael had always loved the many different fragrances that permeated the unspoilt land around the lake but, as he breathed in, the added aroma of his mate made it all the more sweet.

"Come on. There's an area over on the far side that has the best view and is closest to the water." He nodded his head in the direction of his favourite spot and led the way.

After about twenty minutes, they arrived at a little alcove surrounded by a copse of trees thick enough to hide them from view on three sides. The only other visitors at the lake occupied the more open space on the other side, giving them a little added privacy.

"During the winter, some of us in the pack like to come out here to hunt. There's plenty of elk and deer, and the scenery's not half bad either." The man was still staring out at the lake when he laid the backpack against the trunk of one of the trees. "If you've been living on Henry's farm, where did you go hunting? I can't imagine at least one member of the clan not spotting you."

Kaden gave him a sharp, quizzical look. He reached up to feel the ridges of the teeth marks at the base of his neck and was silent for a few minutes.

"Greg… I mean, I was told that I can't shift. I guess it's because of my mage blood."

Michael frowned at him, noticing the slip, but deciding to file it away for later. "Didn't your parents ever discuss it with you?"

Kaden turned so that Michael could only see his profile. From the brief glint of pain he caught on the young man's face, he knew he was broaching a sensitive subject, but denying one's true nature, especially when one was a were, could have serious repercussions.

"My father was a wolf. My mom had never known a were before she met him, and he managed to tell her some things about what it meant to be born with a second nature before he was…" Kaden let out his next words on a gust of breath. "Before he was killed."

Well, shit. Way to start off the picnic, Michael. "I'm sorry. Was it by a clan member?"

There was a short burst of sarcastic laughter. "No. My mom's coven. They didn't take too kindly to her *lowering* herself to choose a were over her own people."

Despite the seriousness of the story, Michael had to hide a brief grin at the level of bitterness and anger in that one sentence. *Kid's got a bite!* "So what happened after that?"

"She packed me and Missy up and we ran. She wasn't sure if her family would turn on us as well, but she didn't want to take the chance. We had to hide and run a lot. My mom… She never did get over the death of my father. I guess she was depressed. I think that's what killed her in the end." Kaden suddenly turned back to glare at him, curling his fists. There was defiance shining in his eyes as he said, "I did what I had to do to support my family.

This time, the boy's anger was decidedly directed at him, and it took him a few confusing moments before understanding came to him.

"The club. You were working there to make money for your family."

Kaden didn't answer Michael. He didn't need to.

Damn, Michael's mother had been right all along about his mate doing what he had to in order to survive. Not that he had doubted her, but the woman could be eerily intuitive at times.

"Kaden, I couldn't have wronged you more. I know you're a better man than I am. The fact that you're willing to give me a second chance proves that. I don't know exactly what happened after our first encounter, but I do want to make sure it never happens again."

He stood facing his mate's scrutiny for several agonising seconds. No apology could suffice for his embarrassing behaviour concerning the boy, but he had to try. After what seemed an eternity, Kaden's muscles relaxed and he unclenched his fists, giving a slight nod of concession.

Michael let out a relieved breath, feeling the tension of the moment pass, but not the shadows from Kaden's eyes. He wanted to reach out to him, comfort him, and the urge to do so soon became an undeniable need.

He walked forward, not stopping until he was only inches away and could feel the heat wafting from the younger man's skin. He could smell his provocative scent, which reminded him of the intimacy they had shared the other morning. Kaden's eyes widened as he traced the movement of Michael's hand as it slowly rose to his face.

Michael hovered his hand just above the man's cheek for several seconds, wanting to give him a chance to pull back if he wasn't ready for his touch, but Kaden didn't move. Finally, he cupped his cheek, marvelling at the softness of his skin and the quickening of his breath. He was able to detect small bursts of emotion, numerous but fleeting.

Desire was easily recognisable, but the others he found harder to read. He could only liken them to feelings he had experienced during certain periods of his life. One emotion reminded him of the time that he had run off and got lost from the rest of his pack following his first shift. He had been terrified then.

Oh no.

"Are you scared of me?" Michael asked gently. The boy ducked his head and his emotions suddenly shifted. They began to fade, and Michael was barely able to make out confusion and…shame?…before they disappeared behind those shadows. He concentrated on filling his being with as much confidence and love as he could. He felt the other man stiffen but Michael pulled him into his arms and held him there before Kaden could move away.

Their embrace was awkward at first. Michael was finding it almost impossible to radiate feelings of comfort while fighting his own demanding arousal. After a few minutes, however, he gradually began to loosen the restraint he held on his emotions when he realised that the man still wasn't responding to him.

He wanted to bring him peace, but they were mates. They should be able to find comfort in their attraction to each other. He wanted his mate to accept all of him, and with that thought, he let go of his inhibitions and poured everything he was feeling into his mate.

The most amazing little sigh came from the mouth resting on his chest and he almost jumped in joy as thin arms wrapped themselves around his tapered waist and squeezed. His cock jerked against the seam of his pants, begging for attention, but this wasn't about him.

He could wait. This was about the hesitant creature he'd longed for over countless nights. He never wanted the moment to end but, all too soon, he felt those arms loosen and slip down, and he reluctantly stepped away, relinquishing his hold.

As empty as his arms suddenly felt, the sight of the bulge in the front of the jeans Kaden wore more than made up for it. A becoming blush and a sexier-than-hell innocent glance of violet eyes through long, blond lashes almost had him coming in his pants. Damn, his mate was gorgeous.

Michael turned swiftly around before he did something a little less than chivalrous and bent to rummage through the backpack. He tossed Kaden a bottle of water and said, "Okay, enough of the past. I only have one and a half more weeks to win you over. Time's a-wastin'."

Kaden let out a burst of laughter as Michael grinned lecherously at him.

"So…what do you have planned now?"

Chapter Five

"Has anyone taught you about Mother Earth yet?" Michael took Kaden's frown as a 'no' and grabbed a bottle for himself. He spent the next several hours exploring the landscape with his mate.

He explained to him that all weres felt a pull to commune with Mother Earth, to establish a relationship with her that would seal a bond that went soul-deep. Once Mother Earth accepted them, became familiar with them, she would give a piece of herself to allow for the shift, just as the shifter gave up a part of his being when he took his other form.

He questioned Kaden as to whether he'd felt urges similar to those that plagued all weres upon reaching adulthood. From his halting admission and description of what he'd experienced in the past, Michael felt confident that the man could indeed shift but wasn't quite ready for it yet.

He told him that they didn't always hunt when they took their wolf forms. Sometimes, when Mother Earth called too strongly for them to resist, they would go on treks that could last days, or even weeks. Most werewolves would remain in their wolf forms for the entire duration, but it was necessary to be aware of which plants could be used for medicinal purposes and how to find fresh water.

At first, Michael was afraid that he might overload his mate with information, but there was quite a bit he was already familiar with, thanks to his sister's power and her insistence that she share her knowledge with him. The enthusiasm with which Kaden seemed to soak up everything else, though, was encouraging.

Michael recalled the endless summer days his father had spent with him, teaching him the same lessons, going over the uses of each plant time and time again, until he had them memorised. Although most of those times had been good, they were nothing compared to the excitement he took in teaching his mate. Kaden's eagerness and innocence made each lesson a new experience for him as well.

And his intelligence was astounding!

Michael supposed that if Kaden had been around seventeen while working in that club, chances were he'd never finished high school. The fact that he now sacrificed so much of his time and money to ensure that his sister received a proper education at home spoke volumes about his dedication to family.

On their hike back down to the little alcove, Michael began to point out plants and berries he had identified on the way up and felt his chest swell with every correct answer Kaden gave. On his best day, when his father had been teaching him, Michael couldn't have retained as much information as his mate had. He complimented Kaden repeatedly and would occasionally touch his arm or cheek to let him know that his words were sincere.

Kaden seemed to glow from the praise. He was once again the kid that had danced with his mom, so carefree, the other morning.

Michael hadn't realised how happy he was that this time *he* had been the one to cause his mate to show so much exuberance until Kaden caught him with a huge, sloppy grin on his face. They had just arrived back when Kaden turned to look at him with a frowning smile.

"What? Why are you looking at me like that?"

Michael felt his grin stretch into a full-fledged smile and shook his head. "You're beautiful. And smart. And this has been the best day of my life since my mom introduced me to her double-chocolate brownies when I was a kid."

Kaden rolled his eyes but kept smiling, which was all that mattered to Michael. He started pulling their shorts from the bag and asked, "Ready to go swimming? The water should be great about now. Afterwards, we can…" Michael cut off his sentence as he saw Kaden hugging himself with a look of fear in his eyes. He immediately dropped the clothes and walked over to him but the man side-stepped out of his reach. "Kaden, what's wrong?"

Kaden hid his face behind his long fall of bangs, a pose Michael was beginning to realise was his way of hiding from the world…or from difficult questions. Michael stepped closer and gently placed two fingers under his chin, lifting his face, but Kaden stubbornly kept his eyes lowered.

"Baby, if I say anything wrong, you've got to let me know. I want to know everything about you, including what you don't like."

"Including my scars?" Kaden whispered.

Michael tried to understand what his mate was getting at, when the answer came to him. "You don't want me to see your scars." Michael could see the barely restrained tears held back by his thick lashes, and pulled him into a hug. "There is nothing about you that I don't find attractive. Those scars may have been made in pain, but they're part of who you are, and I want all of you, not just the good aspects. Besides, if you got those scars because of my neglect, then they should be on my body. Would you think any less of me if they were?"

"No!" The response was immediate. "But you would never let someone do this to you. You're not weak like I am." His soft-spoken words held a wealth of self-contempt and Michael had to rein in his temper, afraid Kaden would mistakenly perceive his anger as directed at him.

Michael pulled away to grip his mate's shoulders. Kaden still refused to look him in the eye. "You. Are. Not. Weak. You're one of the strongest men I've ever met, and you didn't *let* someone do that to you. There will always be another who is stronger and meaner than any of us. It doesn't make us weak, and everyone needs a little protection every once in a while. Even me."

"I'm not strong…"

"Really? How many people do you know can grow up alienated from those that should have protected them, support their families, raise a teenage girl, survive a hell no one should have to endure only to do something productive and kind with a gift that was abused, and still be able to smile? If you think that kind of strength can be found in just anyone, you're wrong."

Kaden shuffled and squirmed out of his grasp. "Please, I just...I can't."

Michael relented, not wanting to push his mate too far. "Okay, no swimming. At least not today." He stepped forward again and bent to kiss Kaden's forehead, then took his hand and led him over to the tree the backpack was laid against. He put the shorts back in and took out the sandwiches he'd packed, handing one to Kaden before leaning back against the tree and starting in on his own.

They ate in comfortable silence, enjoying the heat of the sun and the sound of the wind blowing through the trees. Kaden had only taken four bites when his eyes began to droop closed. Michael suppressed the urge to tell him to eat more, not wanting to take the chance of breaking the pleasant mood, and opened his arms in invitation.

Kaden hesitated at the gesture and chewed adorably at his bottom lip before setting aside his food and laying his head down on Michael's lap. The moment the man's head grazed his crotch, fire raced through his body and he could feel his cock come to life.

It took him several moments to breathe through his sudden arousal, which he was sure Kaden was fully aware of, before he could relax again and enjoy the feel of the slight weight pressing into him.

"Thank you," he said.

"For what?" Kaden asked sleepily.

"For giving me this. For giving me you." He stared down in wonder at the young man he was beginning to admire more and more, for both his strength and his courage. He stroked the blond locks away from his beautiful face and became fascinated with the soft texture of the strands.

After a while, he felt Kaden's breathing even out, indicating he had fallen asleep. He wanted to stay awake to revel in the feel of his mate lying so restfully in his lap, but soon his own eyelids began to droop, and he gave in to the tranquillity of the moment.

* * * *

The sun was setting by the time they arrived back at the house, lighting the clouds afire in vibrant shades of purples, pinks and yellows. He'd kept in constant physical contact with Kaden during the return trip, delighting in every peek of emotion he was able to discern.

It was becoming easier now, but he wasn't sure if that was because of their growing bond or because the smaller man was consciously letting his guard down. Either way, he was grateful for it.

His hand now rested on Kaden's forearm and he squeezed it gently to wake him up as his driveway came into view. The pup must have been exhausted from the past several days' events.

"Wake up, sweetheart. We're home." It felt so good to say that, even if it was a little pre-emptive. Michael parked the truck just as Kaden opened his eyes and blinked blearily at him. "Feel like going to bed, or do you want to stay up and watch a movie? I can order some pizza if you'd like."

The young man furrowed his brow, then opened and closed his mouth several times.

"Kaden? What is it?"

Kaden hesitated for a few more seconds before asking, "Why are you being so nice to me?"

Michael was slightly taken aback by the question, but quickly recovered. "You're my mate." He continued hastily before Kaden could get out the argument he could see forming on his face. "Because you make me feel good. I was a fool when we first met. I thought that being mated would take my independence from me, force me to take on responsibilities I didn't think I was ready for yet, and I didn't give myself the chance to realise what a great person you are. Wait!" he said before the man could voice his next objection.

"Let me finish. When I saw you in that barn, I felt the same fears, but now that I've gotten to know you a little, I don't have those fears anymore. You add to everything I am instead of taking anything away. I also know that you don't believe me yet, but I'm working on that. You promised me two weeks, remember?" He smiled to take the reprimand out of his words and was relieved when Kaden sent him a tentative smile back.

"Now, what's it to be? Movie, or bed?" He waggled his eyebrows suggestively, which brought out the intended light laugh from his mate.

"Movie, please," Kaden said softly.

Michael grinned at his shyness and turned to get out. Grabbing the backpack from the bed of the truck, he led the way to the front door and asked, "What do you want on your pizza?"

"Umm...meat lover's?"

Michael laughed and said, "My kinda man. Meat lover's it is." He moved to allow Kaden to enter first, then locked the door behind him. He usually didn't take such precautions, having a house that was a good mile from the road, but there was still the nasty business of the murder they needed to address, and he wasn't taking any chances. "The DVDs are in the shelves below the television. Why don't you pick something out while I call in for the food?"

Kaden nodded and left while he dialled the only pizza place that delivered this far out and placed the order. He spotted a note from his mom on the kitchen table telling him that she and his father had taken Missy with them to a late barbeque at the Ratchet's home and would be back in time to put her to bed.

Grabbing two sodas from the fridge, he joined his mate in the living room and put the comedy he'd chosen into the DVD player while relaying the information. There wasn't too much concern over the safety of his sister, which meant that his mate was learning to trust his parents.

By the time he was done turning everything on and adjusting the volume, he looked back to see that the man was sitting on the far end of the couch. He sat a few feet away but positioned his body to angle himself towards his mate. "Kaden, I won't touch you if you don't want me to, but if you do, I promise not to try anything tonight. I just love having you close to me."

Kaden nodded his head vigorously, as though wanting to change the subject, and Michael reluctantly turned his head back to the TV but kept his attention on the small form next to him. Five minutes into the movie, he began to notice that whenever the man fidgeted, he would move his body closer to him.

Ten minutes later, he tried to tamp down his excitement when a fine-boned hand touched his thigh, and twenty minutes after that, he had to mask a sigh of contentment as Kaden snuggled into his side and rested his head on Michael's shoulder. All too soon afterwards, the doorbell rang and Michael felt the loss of that delicious heat as the man sat up.

"Pizza guy," he said, and pulled his wallet from the back pocket of his jeans as he rose to answer the door.

Michael paid for the order and stacked some plates from the kitchen atop the box before taking everything into the living room. Watching his gorgeous mate dig in to the pizza was more satisfying than any five-star meal could ever be. The man actually devoured four whole pieces before leaning back against Michael's side on the couch.

Shortly after they'd finished their meal, the doorbell rang again and he glanced at the clock on the VCR. It was a little early to be his parents and he hadn't been expecting any other company.

With a frown, he stood up and said, "I'll be right back. Keep my spot warm."

He caressed Kaden's cheek, noticing that the bruises were gone thanks to the rapid healing abilities of all werewolves, and made his way again to the front door. He opened it, expecting to find one of his Betas, but instead was shocked to see Eileen standing there dressed scantily in a mini-dress and heels. Though it was considerably cool outside, her were blood allowed her body temperature to regulate itself in almost all weather conditions.

"Eileen. Hi. What are you doing here?" He knew exactly what she was doing here dressed like that, but he didn't want to feed into her desires. They'd dated on and off for about a year before Michael had first met Kaden, and even though their breakup had been mutual, she'd been trying to seduce him ever since he had taken his father's place as Alpha of their pack.

He hadn't minded at first, amused by her more outrageous antics, but after the desire for his mate had turned into a burning need to find and claim the man, they had quickly become annoying. He'd tried every polite way to tell her that he wasn't interested anymore, but she knew that he hadn't been with anyone for the past four years and he'd been reluctant to tell her the reason why.

He supposed he was partly at fault for her presence on his doorstep right now. He had yet to tell her – or most members of his pack, for that matter – that he'd found his mate and had no plans to be with anyone else. But he still couldn't bring himself to shut her down rudely.

"Michael," she breathed in a sultry voice, "Are you here alone again? Your mom was telling me the other day that you were feeling kind of lonely, so I thought I might drop by to cheer you up."

The shock of her blatant lie almost made him laugh in her face, but he managed to school his expression into one of blankness. His mom knew very well he wouldn't settle for anyone other than his mate.

"Well, I appreciate your thoughtfulness, but I'm actually a little busy at the moment. I'll call you tomorrow, okay?" He started to close the door, but she wedged the tip of her pointed heel underneath the bottom of the door to stop it and stepped in with her other foot, effectively inviting herself into his house.

"You know, I've been regretting the fact that we never really gave our relationship a chance to grow, and I know you miss me. You've hardly been with anyone else since we broke up the last time."

Michael couldn't retreat fast enough before she pressed her body into his, rubbing her scent and curves along the hard planes of his body.

"Who are you?" a soft, low voice said from behind.

Michael closed his eyes and prayed to Mother Earth to end this nightmare he was in. But it didn't end. He gently pushed Eileen away and turned to face his mate, who had the most adorable expression of jealousy on his face that Michael had ever seen.

Eileen didn't seem to notice the distance he had put between them as she sized his mate up. "I'm his girlfriend." Without pause, she turned back to Michael as though she couldn't be bothered with Kaden's presence and asked, "Who is this scrawny little pup, a stray you picked up? I love that you have such a big heart."

Kaden let out a surprisingly deep growl and launched himself at the offending woman. Michael barely managed to catch him before he could reach her, wrapping his arm around his mate's waist and lifting him a few feet into the air before pulling him back to a safe distance further into the foyer.

"Kaden! I'll explain this later. Right now I need you to return to the living room."

Kaden sent him a look of such outrage that it actually made him proud. In a twisted sort of way, he was ecstatic over the fact that his mate cared about him enough to try to keep away other suitors. Not that Eileen had a snowball's chance in hell.

"No. You're my mate, and I'll be damned if I let some woman shove everything but her pussy in your face while I sit idly by!"

Michael was so shocked by Kaden's words that he barely heard Eileen's sharp bark of laughter.

"Your mate?" She cackled again before saying in an icy tone, "Boy, you may look like a girl, but this *man* is not gay. He's never been with another male in his entire life and you think he's going to give it up for you? Oh, this is too good."

Michael cringed at her callous words and was still holding onto Kaden when he felt the man go absolutely still in his arms. Looking down into his face, he watched as Kaden swallowed convulsively then, slowly, as if in a daze, raised his gaze to search Michael's eyes.

"You're not gay?" he whispered.

Michael wanted to say yes, to deny all of Eileen's hateful words, but he was still touching Kaden and his mate would be able to tell whether he was lying or not. Truthfully, he knew he wasn't gay, had never felt anything for another man in his entire life. But when it came to the gorgeous being in his arms, sexuality no longer mattered.

"No," he replied in a low voice. "I'm not, but you are still my mate."

Eileen — *was she still here?* — let out another snort of laughter which brought Kaden's attention back to her.

"Oh shit, that's the reason you were embarrassed by me, isn't it? It's why you left." Kaden paused for an answer, and it absolutely killed Michael not to be able to deny his accusation. Kaden knew the truth without needing an answer. He could see it in Michael's eyes. Michael saw tears glisten on his lashes before Kaden wrenched his body from his grasp and ran into the kitchen.

He sighed heavily and turned back to the woman still standing in his doorway.

"Michael, what the hell was that all about? And why did you call him your mate?" The sarcasm had left her voice and only concern lined her face now. Apparently her bravado had run out along with the presence of the threat to her desired position as an Alpha's mate.

"Eileen, that man *is* my mate, and from now on, you will give him the courtesy due his position. Now, if you don't mind, I have to try to rectify this disaster with him." He started to veer her out of the door with his body without having to touch her, but she was having none of it.

"You can't be serious. Michael, you're not gay. We fit so well together, even your mom thinks so. Are you pulling this crap to get back at me because I broke up with you?"

Michael could only stare, stunned, until her words finally sank in. When they did, his rage at her lies robbed him of thought for another couple of seconds. Before he could start in on her, he saw his father's SUV making its way towards the house.

He silently sent a prayer of thanks to Mother Earth for their early arrival and a grin broke out on his face as he turned back to Eileen to say, "Well, there's my mom. Perhaps you'd like to have her tell me how much she thinks we should be together?"

The woman's face paled as she swung around to see his father park and get out of the vehicle, his mother helping Missy from the back seat. Eileen swung back with a furious look on her face, knowing her bluff had been called.

"Fine. I lied about your mom, but you can't deny that we would be the best match for our clan to prosper. Are you really going to throw away the livelihood of those that depend on you to prance around with a boy that looks like a little girl?"

Michael didn't even have time to react to that new insult before Katherine bounded up the steps leading to his front door and grabbed Eileen by the throat, hauling her out onto the porch and banging her into the side of the house.

"That's my son you're talking about, *little girl,* and if I ever hear you insult him like that again, I will rip your tongue from your mouth and feed it to you along with your disgusting, little black heart. Do you hear me?" His mom actually raised Eileen half a foot into the air before slamming her back against the wall for emphasis. Her treatment was rough, but wouldn't cause much damage to a were.

His ex-girlfriend barely managed, "Yes, m—ma'am," before she was tossed, one-handed, off the porch, where she landed with her now-torn dress hiked up to her waist, revealing a red backside. Eileen hastily picked herself up and ran as fast as she could back to her car as his mom growled at her with all the fury of a mother protecting her cubs.

Michael had never seen his mom like this and was highly impressed, but waited until Eileen's car had disappeared around the bend in the road before saying, "Damn, Mom. Remind me *never* to piss you off."

As if transforming into a completely different person, she turned to him with a coy look on her face and said, "I just don't take kindly to people out to hurt my sons. Now, where is the other one? I made him and Missy some clothes and I want them to try them on before we hit the sack."

Michael sent his father a bewildered look and gestured towards his mom, but Sam simply shook his head and shrugged. "Never come between a female were and the happiness of her cubs. It's not a pretty sight."

Missy, who had taken in the whole incident with wide, incredulous eyes, now burst into laughter and followed after Katherine. "Wow. That was so cool! Will I be able to do that when I'm older?"

Katherine gave her a conspiratorial smile and breezed past him into the house as if she had not just threatened violent pain to the woman who had insulted his mate. She held out a cloth bag to him that she had previously discarded on the porch.

"Well? Where's my new son?"

Michael took the proffered sack from her hand and placed it on the couch. "He's in the kitchen. Things got a little out of hand even before you showed up."

Katherine raised her eyebrows and asked, "What happened? Is he okay? I swear to Mother Earth, if that vile woman hurt a single hair on his head, I'll tear her…"

"Mom! Geez! And here I thought you were the peacemaker of the family. I'm almost afraid to tell you that it was my fault. Because I haven't told anyone but you two that my mate is male, he thinks that I don't want him. Let me go and try to smooth things over before we join you."

"Go on, son. We'll be out here for a bit, but if he doesn't feel like talking, we'll just see you both in the morning," Sam said.

Michael sent him a grateful look, strode over to his mom to kiss her on the temple, then raced for the kitchen. He'd been desperate to get to his mate ever since he had run from the room. He couldn't wait any longer. Just as he got to the doorway, he stopped to get his emotions under control.

He wanted to touch Kaden, but couldn't risk harming him any more than he already had. After several deep breaths, he walked tentatively into the room and looked around, but couldn't find the slight form of the pup anywhere.

He walked quickly to the guest bedroom Missy was using, then searched the downstairs bathroom only to come up empty. Fear seized his heart as he bounded up to the second floor and looked in his bedroom as well as the adjoining bathroom, both devoid of his mate.

As he reached the head of the stairs, he bellowed, "Dad!" His father reacted instantly, meeting him in the downstairs hallway, alert to the stress in his son's voice.

Michael continued to re-check the entire downstairs as he ground out, "He's not here. Dad, he's gone. I can't find him. Oh Mother, he's on his own. He's…"

Sam had to grab his arm so tightly that he nearly wrenched it out of its socket before he could bring Michael's frantic search to a halt.

"Michael!" he shouted. When his son finally stopped to look at him, he asked, "Was Kaden in the kitchen before we got here?"

Michael had to forcefully slow his breathing until he was able to answer, "He ran in there right before you showed. At least that's what I thought."

"Did you check the back door?"

Michael thought about that and cursed as he realised he hadn't. Running back to the kitchen with Sam close on his heels, he felt his lungs constrict as he saw that the door leading from the kitchen to the back yard was indeed open a few inches.

"Dad, shit. My mate..." He was beyond coherent words as he realised that he had lost his mate again due to his negligence.

Without another thought, he stripped and let the feverish rush of warmth consume him as he reached for his wolf form. The communion of his body and soul with Mother Earth was exhilarating and humbling at the same time. She took his devotion of spirit and allowed her own energy to flow through him, consuming him and giving him the strength he needed to keep the delicate balance between his own consciousness and that of the new form she bequeathed to him. The whole transformation took no more than a second, and he was bounding out of the door in the next.

He shook out his thick coat, rejoicing in the sharpening of his already keen senses this form brought to him, and paused to inhale deeply. His mate's scent was strong, and he immediately headed in the direction of the sweet smell of ocean spray and wild flowers.

He became vaguely aware of Sam flanking his left side as he rushed headlong into the night, leaping over fallen branches and dodging tree trunks in his path. The memory of his mate's carefree laughter from their day spent at the lake rang in his ears, and the pain at the thought of never being able to hear that again almost caused him to collide with a large fir tree, but he swerved at the last moment to narrowly avoid it.

He reminded himself that Kaden would never abandon his sister, which meant that he would have to come back eventually, but that did little to ease the guilt of his latest mistake.

He felt Sam open the mental link they shared as Alphas and heard him say, "*Michael, this direction leads to the ravine. Did you go over the lay of the land with him yet?*"

Fear twined its way around his heart at his father's words. "*No. Dad, he hasn't shifted yet. I don't think his senses are heightened enough to see the edge with so little light.*" Kaden may be part were, but he wouldn't truly develop the advanced senses of a wolf until he merged his soul with Mother Earth. The moon was nearly full but its beams could only partially penetrate the thick canopy of tree leaves and branches above them.

"*Faster, son. I think I see him.*"

The beating of light footsteps on the ground ahead of him had his heart racing and he took another deep breath. The smell of his mate was getting stronger. There, to his right. He caught a glimpse of bare, pale feet streaking ahead of him. They were roughly a mile from the house but he couldn't detect a slowing in his mate's frantic flight. He was close. So close.

"*Faster!*"

That's when he saw the sheer drop. He howled out a loud warning to his mate, but Kaden wouldn't stop. Just yards from the border, his steps faltered and Michael knew he'd finally noticed the difference between the darkness of the land and the black emptiness of open space, but it was too late. Kaden's forward momentum pulled him, stumbling, across the last few feet, and he tumbled over with a frightened cry.

Michael didn't even think twice. He doubled his speed and barely heard the warning growl from his father before he leapt over the edge. He shifted in mid-jump so that after a few seconds of weightlessness, his human form slammed into that of his mate and he wrapped his entire body protectively around the slight frame. Time was suspended as they plummeted together, buffeted by crisp gusts of wind, before tumbling into the raging water below. The force of their fall plunged them into darkness.

Chapter Six

Kaden awoke to the feeling of suffocation. Warmth surrounded him on all sides and a crushing weight seemed to be wrapped around his ribcage. He tried to breathe, but something was covering his face, blocking off precious oxygen.

Memories flooded his mind and he was back in the basement, recovering from his latest beating. A solid, black hood covered his head, secured by a buckle at the back of his neck. There was no room to move...no air. Kaden started to struggle, desperate to get free of his prison. How had Gregory caught him? He'd been so careful. This wasn't happening. Not again.

"Kaden, enough!" a sharp, rumbling voice said, stilling him instantly. The tone of it resonated throughout his back, sending waves of vibrations into his bones. He knew that voice. It was strong and commanding and wrapped him up in a steel embrace that he never wanted to climb out of.

His mate.

The words echoed through his mind before he could fully comprehend their meaning. He could feel the promise of dominance and protection and loyalty in the powerful arms currently squeezing the life out of him. He tried to take a breath to speak, but the man with the death-grip on him from behind only squeezed tighter. He tried struggling again, but it brought the hold around his ribs to the point of pain.

All he could do was whimper his distress. As soon as the sound escaped him, the hold immediately loosened, but still didn't give him a square inch to move around in. Kaden took several deep breaths before trying to talk, but his first word came out as more of a croak. He tried to clear his throat but it felt like he had swallowed sandpaper which was now glued to his vocal cords.

After another attempt, he was racked by a fit of coughing and felt his upper body lifted into a sitting positions. Tears sprang to his eyes and prevented him from seeing the glass of water being pressed to his lips.

He started to brush the object away until that deep voice resounded again, saying, "Drink."

At once, he stopped struggling, as if that voice was connected directly to the synapses of his nerve cells, forcing his body to heed its command. As soon as he felt the rim of the glass tilt forward on his lips and the cool splash of water hit his tongue, he groaned at the renewed life it gave to his parched throat. He gulped down long swallows but, all too soon, the glass was taken away. He couldn't help but reach blindly for it, trying desperately to bring it back to his mouth.

"That's enough for now. Lie back down."

Kaden was pressed back into the softness of the mattress by that overwhelming weight once again, but he had another piece of business to take care of. He opened his eyes slowly and was relieved to find the room he was in blanketed in darkness. He blinked his gritty eyes several times until they felt like they were made out of living tissue again instead of coarse granite.

"Michael?" he whispered.

"What?" The tone was decidedly less than pleasant, but he could feel no anger or negative emotions coming from the man. For that matter, he could discern no emotions whatsoever, but he put off that thought in light of more pressing matters.

"Umm…I need to pee. Think you could maybe let go of…"

"No." The response was deadpan, instant, and in no way negotiable. Kaden was about to argue on his bladder's behalf when he felt the huge man shift behind him and lift him from the bed without allowing a single inch of air to come between them. Pain shot through every muscle in his body and another whimper escaped before he could suppress it. The strength of the embrace never relented, however.

A small lamp on the dresser was flipped on as Michael made his way to the bathroom. As they reached the toilet, the large man gracefully lowered him onto the open seat, then promptly sat to his immediate left on the edge of the bathtub and kept hold of his wrist, never once breaking physical contact.

Kaden sat there, trying to modestly cover his flaccid cock in the dim light, and realised after several seconds that the man was not going to give him any privacy. In fact, Michael was staring at him with a shadowed, stoical look on his face as if they had been discussing some dire issue.

Kaden began to relive the fear that always came at the loss of independence and was about to resort to begging for privacy when Michael sighed, stood up and turned his back to him, all while keeping his wrist in a gentle yet unbreakable hold.

"This is as far as I go. Don't be embarrassed. I'll be using the toilet as soon as you're done," Michael said.

Kaden still couldn't pick up on his emotions, which was a first, but he wasn't about to argue. It was hard enough to have someone holding his hand like a child while he peed, let alone having to feel that person's emotions while doing the deed.

It took him a few minutes before he was able to relax his muscles enough to urinate while being touched, but he finally managed. When he was finished, Michael switched places with him, standing over the toilet and guiding himself towards the bowl with one hand while his other remained on Kaden's wrist.

After flushing the toilet, Michael turned back to him and lifted him up, only to turn around and place him gently onto the countertop next to the sink. The man then situated his large body between Kaden's thighs and reached over to open the mirror cabinet next to his head, searching the contents until he found what he was looking for and pulled out a white bottle with black lettering on it.

Kaden began to feel extremely uncomfortable. He couldn't detect a single emotion from the man and couldn't understand why he was being so overbearing. He also didn't know why his entire body ached with every movement.

"Michael, what…"

"Take these." Michael pressed two tiny white pills into his hand and poured water into a small, disposable cup which he placed into his other hand.

"Michael. Did I do something wrong? Please…"

Michael gently lifted Kaden's hand, carrying the two pills to his mouth until Kaden was forced to place them on his tongue and quickly take a swig of water to swallow them down and wash away their acrid taste.

The large man silently took the cup from his hand and lifted him into his arms again, turning directly around and setting him on his feet outside the bathtub. He pulled a corner of the shower curtain open and reached around to turn on the spray and adjust the temperature. Kaden felt his body begin to tremble in fear as the man touching him remained emotionally unresponsive.

Michael's cold, unfeeling behaviour was beginning to remind him of Gregory even though, logically, he knew he was not the same as the monster who had tormented him for years. The loss of the tentative connection he was sure had been growing between them hurt more than he would have thought possible. His breathing began to quicken and he tried one more time to break through the emotional barrier Michael had erected between them.

"Michael, please. Whatever I did, I'm sorry. Are you punishing me?"

That got the man's attention. He tightened his hold around Kaden's wrist to near pain, then scooped him up again and walked them both into the shower. Michael slowly lowered him to the floor until the massaging stream of water hit his back, soothing and stinging at the same time.

"Mich—ael." His voice broke and he knew he couldn't take it if this man used him the same way he'd been used in the past.

Michael cupped his cheeks in a tender embrace that belied his apathetic emotional response and raised his face until their eyes met and locked.

As Michael slowly lowered his body to kneel before him, Kaden gradually began to feel what he was keeping inside, which he had somehow managed to disguise from him. Feelings seeped into him like twisting tendrils of smoke. He could recognise sadness, longing, and a desperation so profound that it took his breath away.

Michael wrapped his long arms around his hips, leaned his head forward onto his chest, and began to weep silently. Kaden thought the despair flowing in waves from the man might drown him, but somehow, Michael was able to regulate its strength even as he sobbed against Kaden's body as if he might fall apart.

Kaden was so astonished by this that he forgot about his fears and placed his hands on the soft, wavy locks of black hair, digging his fingers in gently to massage Michael's scalp. His own confusion warred with the racking pain surging from the man who was shaking so hard against him he was afraid he might shatter.

Kaden had never been in the position of the comforter, except when caring for his sister. He had even less experience at being comforted himself. The feel of such a powerful man kneeling and weeping against him brought out all of his protective instincts. He had no idea what had brought this on, but found himself unable to retain any vestiges of reluctance to care for the man weeping silently against him.

Kaden bent forward and wrapped his arms around Michael's head, trying to offer whatever solace he could in a situation that completely baffled him.

Time was only measured by the force of Michael's tortured sobs as he held on to Kaden as though he were his only lifeline to reality. Eventually, his sobs turned to fitful, shuddering breaths, which in turn ended until there was nothing left to expend.

Soft lips tickled Kaden's belly as Michael asked in a hoarse voice, "You don't remember any of it, do you? The doctor said you might have some memory loss."

Kaden searched his brain for any clue as to what he was talking about, but could find nothing. "Did I do something wrong?"

Michael let out a breathy gust of laughter and tilted his head up to fix his hazel gaze on him. There, on his knees, Michael began to relate the occurrences of a few nights ago. Kaden shook his head in emphatic denial.

"That can't be. My life may not be worth living at times, but I've never wanted to kill myself. I have Missy and…" He wanted to say 'you', but was still uncertain about their relationship. "I wouldn't do that on purpose. I wouldn't…"

"I know, baby. That's one of the things I love about you. You're stronger than that. I didn't tell you about the ravine and your eyesight isn't sharp enough yet in the dark. You never saw it coming. I'm so sorry, baby."

Kaden didn't even realise he had started to back away until Michael tightened his embrace, saying, "Don't. I still have one week left, and I'll probably be a little overbearing and you'll have to forgive me for that, but I can't let go of you. I need to touch you, to feel that you're here with me. Is that okay?"

Kaden was still reeling from the story of the events Michael had related to him. No matter how hard he tried, he could only remember as far as falling asleep on the man's lap out at the lake they had visited. Something about the story, though, had him worried more than anything else.

"Michael, if you're not gay, do you...do you wish I was a girl? Female?"

"What?"

"If I...if I were female, would you be able to love me then?" Kaden stammered.

He wasn't sure if what he was asking was fair to the man. Michael had admitted that he had rejected Kaden partly because he was male, but he seemed to be putting forth the effort of getting past that fact now. While Kaden knew no one in their right mind would want him, because of his mixed blood and because of the marks Gregory had left with his whips, claws and teeth, he still didn't want a mate to have to settle for him.

He couldn't change his gender, and he couldn't imagine waking up each morning to see the look of disappointment on his mate's face when he was reminded that Mother Earth had given him a male mate.

Michael stood up. Kneeling, his head had reached Kaden's chest—standing, he towered impressively over him.

Placing his large hands on either side of Kaden's head and tilting it up, Michael said, "I don't know if what I'm feeling is love—I've never been in love before—but I do know that I don't want anyone but you. After I met you, I thought about the women I've slept with…"

A low growl issued forth from Kaden's throat and his upper lip curled into a snarl before he could stop himself, which drew a short laugh from Michael. "Easy, pup. There was never any competition. Once I met you, you were all I saw, every day. Your face, your body. And most especially, this."

Michael reached down with one hand and grasped Kaden's limp cock, squeezing and pumping it a few times until it grew as hard as steel. Kaden let out a gasp of shock and his eyes widened in wonder. Michael continued to slide his hand slowly, from base to tip, along his shaft.

"There has been no one but you these past four years, and there never will be again."

Kaden watched as the man leant down to capture his lips, sliding his tongue seductively along them and delving inside the moment he opened up. Michael's taste was every bit as heady as he remembered. He drank in as much of the arousing taste as he could and had to wrap his hands around the thick biceps surrounding him as he felt the room tilt.

A gentle thumb feathered across his cheek in a soft caress before the palm it belonged to moved to the base of his head, holding him there, giving him no chance to escape.

"I want all of you, baby." Michael bent his knees until his own cock, already engorged with blood and weeping pre-cum, was level with Kaden's, then opened his hand to grip both of them. The sensations of the water hitting their cocks, the warmth of their skin touching, and the friction caused by Michael's hand that never stopped pumping, had them both groaning. Kaden began to thrust his hips frantically, but the larger man took complete control, setting his own languid, excruciating pace.

"Your cock." Michael gave a particularly rough tug that caused Kaden to gasp and sent a shiver through his entire body. "Your perfect ass. Your sweet smile." Kaden's bottom lip was sucked into that demanding mouth before Michael bit down with just enough force to cause a stinging pain that made the swirl of his tongue across it all the more electrifying.

The slow pace of the man's firm hand on their cocks was beginning to drive Kaden insane. He could feel a deep pressure building in him that had all the muscles in his body tensing and releasing, but he needed more. He lowered his hands to Michael's hips and dug his fingers into them, raking his nails down his buttocks and moaning when he felt him shudder.

"Your laugh. The way you make me feel." The strokes began to quicken as Michael kissed his way down to his neck, where he licked at the mating mark. Kaden trembled and started to whimper pleadingly as a tingling sensation raced down his spine, letting him know that his orgasm was imminent. Michael pumped them both harder and faster and said fiercely, "Come, boy. Come for me."

That deep, commanding voice sent him over the edge and he felt his balls tighten just before his release shot out of him. He dropped his head back, screaming his mate's name, unable to keep in the powerful, rocking force of his pleasure. It blinded him and made him hyper-aware of the hard, glorious body pressed so intimately into him as he trembled with pleasure.

Moments later, Michael let out a loud growl and jerked against him as he found his own release. With the steam in the shower and the haze of their forceful orgasms still clouding their minds, it seemed as if they were floating in their own little world. The large hand never stopped pumping until they were both soft again. Kaden's body went limp and he was sure he would have melted into the floor if not for the strong arm encircling him, holding him close.

"I never want to let you go, baby," Michael whispered, bowing to kiss the top of his head.

Michael heard a muffled sigh from his mate and chuckled. Turning Kaden to the side and leaning him against the wall, he asked, "Can you stand for me?"

Kaden offered a weak nod, but Michael made sure his knees were braced before reaching over to grab the bottle of body wash and pouring a good portion into his hand. He began to wash his mate's body, starting with his neck and shoulders. When his fingers rubbed over the mating mark, he felt Kaden's body shiver and he couldn't stop the grin that curved his lips.

There were still a few bruises marring his chest and legs where he had been battered against the rocks beneath the water at the bottom of the ravine. Michael had tried to cover as much of his body as he could, but after they had crashed into the water, Kaden had struck his head on a boulder jutting out from the edge and had immediately lost consciousness.

It had been almost impossible to hold on to every part of the boy's limp body as they had been tossed about by the shifting currents.

He'd remained conscious, but had suffered several scrapes in his effort to hold on to his mate. They were inconsequential, however, considering the fact that, had he taken just a few more seconds in discovering that his mate was gone, he wouldn't be holding him, caring for him, right now.

When he got to the boy's now slack cock, he heard a moan and watched it begin to rise again as he spread the body wash over it, thorough in his attention. His mouth watered as he realised he had yet to taste the long, thin spear rising under his ministrations, but there would be time for that later. He had no intention of letting Kaden out of his reach for as long as he could justify it, let alone out of his sight.

He moved down to his legs and feet, rubbing lightly over the abraded skin and massaging the muscles. Standing up again, he poured more soap into his hands and gave the younger man a brief kiss.

"Turn around."

Lazily, Kaden turned and raised his arms to the wall, resting his head on his forearms as Michael began to wash his back. He was glad that his mate was no longer self-conscious about his scars around him, and he worked to keep the thoughts of how they got there from affecting his emotions.

Tomorrow, he would need to encourage Kaden to tell his story. If he knew the killers, Michael would need to know what his association with them was, and he had a feeling that it was connected to his scars, but that was tomorrow. Today, he wanted to lavish his mate with as much attention and love as he could.

After aiming the spray to rinse the soap from his mate and turning him around again, he poured a dollop of shampoo into his hand and lightly applied it to the man's scalp. A small whimper sounded from Kaden's lips as his fingers grazed over the knot on the back of his skull.

"I'm sorry, baby. You hit your head pretty hard, but I've got to wash out any blood left there." He felt his chest tighten as the other man nodded his head and pressed his thin body against him, wrapping his arms around his waist and tucking his face into the hollow of his neck.

It showed an amount of trust that made his eyes sting with new tears, but he blinked them back and pointed the shower nozzle so that the water cascaded over Kaden's hair and down his body.

When Michael was finished, he quickly washed his own body, keeping himself as close to his mate as possible. Afterwards, he turned the water off and grabbed a towel from the shelf above the toilet to blot the water from his mate's soft, pale skin before drying himself off. Kaden's eyes were half-lidded as Michael scooped him up and carried him back into the bedroom.

"I can walk, you know," Kaden said in a teasing voice.

Michael shifted him in his arms so that he could grab his own clothes from hangers in the closet, then picked up a green, cloth bag from the top of the dresser before settling Kaden onto the foot of the bed.

"I know you can. Just humour me." Michael knelt down in front of the sexy man and held out the bag to him, answering his questioning look simply by telling him to open it. Kaden looked inside, then pulled out two pairs of slacks, one blue, the other black, along with a black, long-sleeved, button-down shirt and a red T-shirt. There were also unopened packages of boxers and socks at the bottom.

"You got these for me?" Kaden asked with a frown.

"As much as I'd like to take the credit, they're from my mom. Read the note."

Another glance inside the green bag revealed a small, cream-coloured envelope. Setting aside the clothes, Kaden took out the card inside and read the elegant scroll written in pen.

For my new son, Kaden,

I hope these fit you. I'm in the process of making more, so if you have any preferences, please let me know. We have been looking forward to having you as a part of our family for years, and now that I've met you, I feel wonderful knowing that my Michael is in such good hands.

All my love,
Mom

Kaden continued to stare at the note for so long that Michael began to get worried. He could smell the tears before he saw them glisten on his mate's long lashes.

"Your mom made these?" he asked quietly.

Michael cupped a hand over his cheek and said, "Our mom made them. She's crazy about you, you know."

"But...but...she only just met me, and I've made so many mistakes... I must seem like a total loser."

Michael let out a sharp bark of laughter. "You think she dances around the kitchen listening to country music with just anyone? I'm the only one she's ever done that with, and that was only until I reached the age of eleven and became too embarrassed and self-absorbed to indulge her. You've made her a very happy woman. You and Missy. They've been cooking up a storm over the past few days. This keeps up and I'll have to invest in a second fridge."

A single tear slipped free but Kaden wiped it away and asked, "You've been looking for me for years? You told your parents about me?"

Michael felt pain engulf his chest as he replied, "Of course. I went back to that club every night for six months, then wrote to every clan I could find. But I should have told the rest of my clan about you. I'm sorry for that. It wasn't that I was ashamed of you, it was just that I'd only met you briefly and, after a while, you started to seem more like a dream that I couldn't make come true instead of a reality. I can't seem to stop making mistakes with you, but I promise I will always try to make up for them, if you'll let me."

Two more tears trickled down his cheeks and, if not for the hand he kept on Kaden's face, allowing him to gauge his feelings, Michael would have thought he'd screwed up again. It tore him apart to watch his mate cry for any reason, but as far as he could tell, these tears reflected happiness, not sorrow.

"I know that nothing I say is going to convince you of the fact that what I feel for you is real and permanent, but for however long it takes, I'll be here, and I won't give up." He made sure to put all of his sincerity into his emotions as well as his eyes.

"Now get dressed. It's about lunchtime and I think I smell hamburgers, which means mom knows we're awake and is expecting us." Michael grinned and kissed his mate on the forehead before reluctantly removing his hand to allow him to get dressed.

They both donned shirts, underwear and pants, but forewent socks and shoes. Michael had no intention of going anywhere that day where he might be required to relinquish physical contact with his mate. As soon as they were ready, he grabbed something from the nightstand, stuffed it into his pants pocket, then swiftly lifted Kaden into his arms and headed out of the room.

"Are you going to carry me everywhere?" Kaden asked wryly.

Michael looked into those vibrant, nearly violet eyes and replied in a solemn tone, "Yes. Mine. For as long as I can keep you." The levity in his eyes belied his serious demeanour. Michael took him downstairs where the smell of food grew stronger and its aroma caused Kaden's stomach to growl.

As Michael entered the kitchen, he saw Sam sitting at the table and his mom hovering over a skillet on the stove. Missy had practically squeezed her entire little body into a bottom cabinet, obviously looking for something that was hiding from her.

His father looked up and smiled as Michael took the seat across from him, adjusting Kaden's weight in his lap and encircling his arms around his small waist. Katherine turned at the noise and also smiled broadly.

"Well, there you two are." She walked over and placed her hands on their heads, kissing each of them on the cheek before returning to the stove to flip the burgers she was cooking. "Kaden, I figured you were roughly about my size, but if the pants don't fit, I can let them out."

Before Kaden had a chance to thank her, Missy sprang from her position on the floor and barrelled into him with a little too much enthusiasm. At the man's grunt of pain, Michael reached around and rubbed the teenager's arm.

"Take it easy on him for a little while, okay? It'll still take him another day or two to heal completely."

Missy immediately stepped back but retained her excited grin. "I'm so happy you're finally awake. Do you like the clothes? I helped Katherine make them. She's teaching me how to sew, and it's really fun! Not as fun as cooking, though. I actually taught her a new recipe, although she has way better ones. Did you get the herbal medicine I made for you?"

"Hi, Missy. And no. Where did you put it?"

Missy turned a fierce glare on Michael. "Grrrrr..."

He was so surprised at the snarl that came from such a sweet-looking girl that he didn't know whether to laugh or run and hide. "Umm...I may have forgotten it in the room, but I promise I'll see that he gets it tonight."

"Oh, you'd better. Now, I have work to do. Gotta go." With that, she pecked Kaden on the cheek and span around to finish whatever task she'd been working on when they came into the kitchen.

Michael turned an incredulous look on Kaden, who only laughed and said, "Don't let her sweet face fool you. She can get mean when she wants to."

Sam grunted. "Great. Two females that could liquefy a man's backbone in two words or less."

"With relish," Michael added.

They fell into a companionable silence then as they watched the women bustle about the kitchen, making entirely too much food for five people. It was mesmerising the way they worked so well together. After a while, he even began to notice a routine in their actions. Missy always seemed to know which ingredients were needed next, and Katherine helped her by opening drawers and cabinets while watching the food.

Kaden leaned close to his ear to whisper, "Your mom's hot!"

He could tell that the man had only meant it for his hearing, but his voice hadn't been nearly low enough. Sam burst out laughing so hard that he almost choked on the swallow of water he'd been sipping from his glass. Michael joined him, throwing his head back and practically howling out his amusement at Kaden's unexpected words.

He looked up to see if his mom had also heard the hushed words. *Yup.* She turned on the sink faucet, grabbed the nozzle of the sprayer beside it, and shot a stream of water at Sam, causing him to sputter in surprise. Michael started laughing harder at seeing his father get soaked, until the spray turned on him, missing Kaden completely.

Katherine locked gazes with Kaden and displayed a grin so wicked that the pup started laughing as well. He and his dad were still chuckling when she turned the water off and picked up the spatula she was using to flip the burgers.

"Now what brought that on?" Michael asked.

Kaden shrugged. "I'm gay, not blind."

Michael and Sam laughed again and Katherine turned back, waving the spatula threateningly at them.

"You two could learn a lesson from him. I'm liable to keep the cherry pie we made for dessert for just us three," she said, waving the utensil to encompass herself, Kaden and Missy. Michael and his father shut up immediately, but couldn't wipe the smiles from their faces. "Mmm-hmm." Katherine turned back to the food with a little swing in her hips this time.

Katherine brought the food to the table and when Kaden tried to move to the empty chair beside them, Michael once more held him in place and gave him a stern look. Without skipping a beat, he began loading food onto a plate for Kaden, not missing the smile that curved Missy's lips as she took in his actions.

He could feel a slight pang of frustration from his mate, but it quickly disappeared as the man attacked his food. The table was filled with chatter throughout the meal, though Missy contributed most of it, and for once, Kaden's plate was empty by the end of it.

"I'm glad you got your appetite back," Michael said.

Sam spoke up from the sink where he was washing his plate. "I'm going to head out to finalise the paperwork Mrs O'Neily needs to expand her lands. I'll have my cell phone with me if you need anything."

"And Missy and I are going to run to the store to pick up some more material. I'm working on Mora's gown for her celebration party. I told you she finally got mated, right?" Katherine asked Michael.

He nodded and smiled. "To Richard, right? He's a lucky wolf."

"Yeah, well… I swear that woman is in full panic mode. She's so nervous she's changed the design of her dress as well as the dresses of her mom and girlfriends—all of which, by the way, I need to have done in the next two weeks—three times already My heart goes out to the poor party coordinator. I can just imagine what he's going through."

Michael laughed and called out his goodbyes. Kaden made sure that Missy was keeping up with her homework online, then gave her and Katherine a kiss goodbye, remembering to thank her for the clothes she'd made. After hearing the front door close,

Michael kept a firm hold of the man's hand as he started gathering their dishes and taking them to the sink.

Much to his chagrin, he found that he had to release the hand in order to clean up, but managed to keep his mate close to him at all times. Kaden was helping him, and from the brief times their fingers touched, he started to feel what he thought was confusion and something else from the boy.

"Kaden, is something bothering you?"

Kaden looked up in embarrassment before shrugging a shoulder and returning his attention to the cup in his hand, scrubbing it a little too vigorously.

"Kaden, I can feel your emotions, remember? I know something is wrong. Tell me."

Kaden huffed, blowing strands of blond hair from in front of his face. "Do werewolves marry? Is that the party your mom was talking about?"

Michael paused at that and set down the towel he was using to dry the dishes. He turned to his mate and took the cup from his hands to set it on the counter, then took both hands in his so that they had no distractions.

"Baby, is that really what's bothering you?"

Kaden blushed, but Michael sensed a thread of anger, and maybe hurt, in him. "I was just curious. I still don't know very much about clans, werewolves…us."

Michael pursed his lips but decided to let the younger man set his own pace for the conversation. "We don't get married, that's a human custom. When we mate, we mark each other," Michael ran a finger across the raised ridges of his mating mark on the man's neck, smiling a little when he saw a shiver run through Kaden's body at his touch, "and that lets everyone know we're taken. We can also tell by the mating scent. Anyone who gets close enough will be able to smell my scent on you, and vice versa."

Kaden frowned. "Then what is the party for?"

"It's a celebration to which the entire clan is invited so that everyone can know that the couple has found each other. Matings don't happen very often and, when they do, it's a joyous event. My clan is very large, like a community, so we use the mating celebrations to mingle with each other, as well as with other clans if one person in the couple happens to come from a different clan. Richard, for example, is from the Wysek clan. They'll be joining us at the party and, hopefully, the mix of wolves will produce more matings."

Kaden's frown deepened as he asked tentatively, "If we were mated, would we... I mean...would you..." He paused and took a deep breath as if gathering his courage. "Would there be a celebration for us?"

Chapter Seven

Michael stood frozen in place, trying to grasp the scope of — and motivation behind — Kaden's question. They were already mated, but the man seemed to equate mating with the mutual consent of both people in a couple.

While he'd heard of matings that had ended in life-long separation, they were extremely rare and never turned out well for either of the couple. It was next to impossible for a wolf to desire another sexually after being mated, and the notion that his own mate might reject him had given him a whole new respect for what Kaden must have suffered when he had been so crudely denied.

But he chose to see Kaden's question as a ray of hope. If he was considering the possibility of a gathering to celebrate their union, then that must mean that he was also entertaining the idea of staying with him. Making a life together.

Before he let his excitement at the prospect overcome his doubts, he said, "Yes. If you chose to stay with me, I would throw the largest celebration my clan has ever seen—or the smallest, depending on what you want. Mom might have some objections to a small party—I think she's been planning my celebration from the moment I was born—but it would be all about you. Whatever you want." He paused, noticing that the frown had not lessened on his mate's face. "Is that what you want?"

Kaden stared into his eyes, searching for something, though he had no clue as to what. "You wouldn't be ashamed of me? Aside from the fact that I'm a guy, and I'm gay, your Betas know I used to sell myself, and…"

Michael cut him off with a kiss, not knowing what to say but unwilling to let the man carry on with his doubts and excuses. It started out as impulsive and abrupt, but as soon as Kaden's sweet taste burst across his tongue, it took on a more languid yet insistent feel. He took his time exploring the caverns of his mouth, biting and licking, loving the soft little moans that came from the back of the man's throat.

"How are you feeling? Still very sore?" He breathed the words in between swipes of his tongue.

"Nope. Can't feel a thing."

Michael chuckled at that while continuing his assault. By the time he broke their kiss, they were both breathing heavily. "I need to be inside you, baby. I need to make love to you. To know that you're mine. I want everyone to know that you're mine." He ripped open the shirt hiding his mate's delicate body from him, causing buttons to fly in all directions, and groaned as that beautiful chest and pale skin were laid bare for him to feast on.

He took one tiny, pink nipple into his mouth and rolled the tip between his teeth, delighting in the surprised gasp that came from his boy. He lavished it with attention until it was swollen and hard, then turned to the other one, biting down with enough force to pull another gasp from his mate.

"Tell me you want this, baby. I have to know. I need to know if you want me. If you want my cock in your ass." He made his way up Kaden's chest, kissing every inch of skin his hands missed, taking care to avoid his fading bruises and scrapes.

This wasn't exactly the best idea considering his mate's condition, but the thought that he'd almost lost him permanently made him feel the need to possess him, devour him. He almost lost himself in the feel of so much soft, tender skin, the thrilling sounds of his mate's excited moans, but he was still waiting for his answer.

He pulled his head back right before he got to Kaden's succulent mouth and asked, "Baby?"

Kaden's blue-violet eyes were half-lidded and Michael could feel the boy's arousal beating at him, trying to take over his control, but he had to know if his mate wanted this as much as he did. "Baby, do you want me?"

"Yes," Kaden whispered vehemently. "Fuck me, now. Please."

That was all the encouragement Michael needed. He crashed his lips over Kaden's and delved his tongue into every crevice he could reach while undoing the button and zipper on the man's pants before shoving them down. Kaden cried out as Michael took his cock in a strong grip and squeezed it just below the head.

The sound of Kaden's pleasure almost had him coming in his pants, but he bit down on the inside of his cheek to stop his impending orgasm and released Kaden's cock. He was so overcome with the need to get inside his boy that his hands trembled as he reached into his pants pocket for the bottle of lube he'd grabbed from the nightstand in his room earlier.

He swiftly undid the buttons of his jeans with one hand, releasing his cock and allowing his pants to fall to the floor before stepping out and kicking them away. With his other, he snapped open the bottle and squirted the liquid straight onto his cock before closing the lid and throwing it onto the counter. He slicked the lube up and down and kept his gaze on his mate's face, watching for any signs of doubt.

Michael lifted the lithe figure to his chest and said, "Wrap your legs around me." Kaden complied instantly and he moved them to the closest wall he could find before leaning the man's back against it and positioning his cock at Kaden's tight, puckered entrance.

He paused as he remembered he hadn't prepared the smaller man's ass to take him. He was about to turn around to retrieve the bottle of lube when Kaden said breathlessly, "No, please. Don't stop. I'm ready."

"I don't want to hurt you."

Kaden took the decision out of his hands when he reached between them and took hold of Michael's cock, guiding it back to his hole and slowly lowering himself onto it. Kaden hissed and he could feel the brief flare of pain through him as Michael's wide cock stretched him impossibly, but he didn't stop. Every inch the man took into him caused the sensitive flesh around his hole to spasm and it heightened Michael's own senses until his world consisted only of the man in his arms.

He could feel Kaden's pleasure invading every part of his being until he lost his individuality. The pain combined with the intense ecstasy he could feel rippling through his mate was like an unstoppable flood and he felt himself falling into the powerful embrace of their combined arousal.

Michael grunted when his balls finally made contact with Kaden's ass, pausing to give his mate time to adjust to his girth. He could feel sweat dripping down his face as he tried to keep from moving, but after a few seconds the man clenched his inner muscles so tightly it drew a cry from him and forced his hips to move involuntarily.

He pulled himself out, then rammed into the man so hard Kaden's back hit the wall with a bruising force. The pleasure that surged through their emotions and ricocheted back and forth between them stole Michael's will from him. He lowered his hands to Kaden's hips and forced his mate to take all of him, pummelling into his ass so strongly that all that could be heard was the slapping of flesh on flesh.

Kaden's eyes rolled to the back of his head and Michael knew he was hitting his gland when the man's pants turned to cries that grew louder with each thrust. He could feel his balls tightening and it took every ounce of his control to hold his orgasm back. He tilted the narrow hips in his hands so that he could drive himself deeper, harder. Kaden suddenly grabbed his hair and screamed just before his cock exploded, spurting jets of pearl-white cum onto their chests.

Michael continued to pound into him ferociously until the contractions of the muscles squeezing his cock came to be too much. He felt his canines lengthen and sank them into Kaden's neck as he thrust one last time into that tight hole, filling it completely with his release. The blood that splashed into his mouth drew out his orgasm until he thought he would pass out. His entire body trembled with the intensity of their passion and he distantly heard Kaden mumble something unintelligible.

Michael collapsed forward and gulped in air as he tried to force his fingers to loosen their grip on the man's hips. His body continued to jerk with aftershocks. Once he was able to lift his head, he captured Kaden's mouth and poured all of his emotions into the kiss. His joy at having his mate alive and well in his arms, his gratefulness for being able to experience something he thought might have forever been lost to him, his love for the strong being that had without a doubt become his entire world.

Love. There was no mistaking it.

"I love you, Kaden," he whispered against those soft lips. "I love every part of you. Your kindness. Your strength. Your sexy body." He encircled the trim waist in his arms, even as he felt himself slipping from the warmth of the man's ass. "I don't care about your past. You did what you had to do to survive. I'm the one who failed you, and I'll be eternally sorry for that."

Michael saw tears forming in his mate's eyes and said, "Kaden? What is it, baby? I can feel your pain. Did I say something wrong?"

Kaden sniffed and laid his forehead against his shoulder. "No, what you said was great. Perfect. But you don't know everything about me. You don't know what he..." Kaden's voice hitched and he bit his lip to keep from blurting out whatever it was he thought would drive Michael away.

Michael lowered him until his feet were touching the floor and braced his hands on either side of Kaden's face, lifting it until those luminous, deep blue eyes were staring into his. "We'll cross that bridge when we get there. For now, I want you to think about what you want to do for the rest of the day. Anything you want."

Michael wiped the moisture from his mate's lashes and smiled when he felt Kaden's mood lighten and his brow furrow as he concentrated on his answer. The excitement that suddenly rushed from the man into him and the way Kaden began bouncing up and down had him laughing and saying, "Okay, I'm guessing you thought of something you want to do. Tell me, sweetheart."

"Can we go to Henry's ranch? I miss the horses I'm training for him, and I don't want him to think I quit, although I don't think I'll be able to go back to work there after what happened. But maybe I could say goodbye. Do you think he'll be mad? Never mind, I shouldn't go. I don't want to put Missy in danger. Besides, I'm sure he's already hired someone else to..."

Michael shook his head and gave up trying to follow Kaden's erratic thoughts. He leant down and kissed those busy lips long enough to make sure he had the young man's attention. As he stepped away to pick up their discarded pants, he said, "You don't have to quit, and I'm almost positive Henry hasn't hired anyone to take your place yet. If you really can communicate with animals, you've got to be one of his most valued employees there. Even if you decide to stay with me, I know Henry, and I'm sure we would be able to work something out so that you can keep your job. I would never take that away from you now that I know how much it means to you."

Michael laid the pants over one arm and scooped his mate up, absently amazed at how well he fitted against him, as if Kaden had been made for him alone. "As for what happened, we'll work that out later. It's my duty to keep you safe *and* happy, and I'll find a way to do that, no matter how many people I have to kill to get you there."

He growled out that last part. The sudden laughter that erupted from Kaden was so pure and carefree that he almost stumbled on his way up the stairs. That was it, right there. That was what he wanted for the rest of his life, and he vowed right then to make sure that sound came out of his mate's mouth every day for as long as he lived.

"So we can go? You don't think he'll be too mad?" Kaden asked, still giggling.

Michael didn't want to. He thought it was quite possibly one of the worst ideas in the world.

He could minimise the risk to Kaden and Missy by taking extra muscle with them and visiting during a time of day when all of the workers should be out in the fields. What had him concerned was the possibility that Kaden would want to stay. And he had no doubt in his mind that should Missy decide she wanted to return there, Kaden would do so for her sake.

"We can go tomorrow. It's a little too late today. I'll call my Betas so they can come as well. I don't want to take any chances that the killers might still be lurking around there, looking for you."

Michael set his mate down on the bathroom counter then turned to start the water for their shower. Kaden looked down at his now-buttonless shirt and frowned.

"So umm...what are you going to say to your mom when you tell her she needs to replace the buttons on this?"

Michael glanced back and had the modesty to blush, but he cleared his throat and said, "Our mom, and you're going to tell her. It is your fault, after all."

"My fault!" Kaden exclaimed indignantly but with a smile on his face.

Michael pulled the shower curtain closed after making sure the temperature was right, then turned to his mate with a sly grin curving his lips. "Hell yeah. If you weren't so damned tempting, I wouldn't have to rip off your clothes every time I kiss you. Better yet, I'm thinking you should just stay naked all the time once the folks leave. Less stress on Mom and all that."

Kaden threw his head back and captivated Michael again. The boy's laugh was so cheerful, it took the world away until there was only the two of them.

* * * *

Michael opened the front door to Dennis and Nick and gave them both a nod of greeting before tugging on his mate's hand to pull him from the house. He could feel the man's nervousness beating at him and knew it must be due to the presence of his Betas, but it was understandable. He hadn't spent very much time in their presence since coming here.

"Wow, you look a lot better. I hope you don't mind, but after we heard about what happened, we came over to check in on you. You had everyone worried," Dennis said.

Kaden's eyes widened at the unexpected attention, then slanted in anger as his slight frame began to shake with emotions so strong, Michael was having a hard time differentiating them.

"You don't have to pretend to be nice to me. We all know I was a whore and that you don't approve of me." Michael saw the man swallow forcibly and inch his body closer to him before continuing. "But don't worry, I promise I won't embarrass your Alpha any more than I already have."

Whether Kaden was quaking from anger or pain, Michael couldn't tell, but he felt his own anger rise up at Kaden's words. His mate had nothing to be ashamed of, unlike himself. He was about to grind out a frustrated objection but Dennis beat him to it.

"Michael, wait." He held up a hand to stop him but never took his eyes from Kaden's face. "You're right. I was worried at first that you weren't the best choice for my Alpha. But after seeing the stress he's been carrying for years after he fucked up…" He glanced at Michael and said, "No offence, but you did," then turned back to Kaden. "Seeing it disappear just from having you around, I'm grateful to you. I can't think of a better mate for my Alpha than a man who not only brings him peace, but is also strong enough to risk himself by testifying against killers. That takes some guts."

Kaden shook his head in denial.

"I'm assuming that because you're still here, you're giving my Alpha a second chance when you could have just told us who the killers were days ago. I can't say that I would be strong enough to risk my heart after being rejected the way you were. Honestly, you amaze me." Dennis raised a hand and held it out, palm side up, to Kaden. "I want to show how sorry I am for wronging you, and that I'm telling you the truth, if that's okay."

Kaden looked from the man's face to his hand, then back again. Dennis's expression was completely open, hiding none of shame he was professing to, but Kaden still seemed hesitant to touch the man in order to gauge his intent. He looked up at Michael with a questioning gaze and Michael nodded to him, trying to tell him that he trusted his Beta's gesture. Kaden took a deep breath and stretched out his hand, laying it in the much larger one of the man in front of him.

Michael watched as Kaden's eyes widened again and felt his anger melt away.

"Kaden?" Michael asked from behind him.

Smiling weakly, he looked into Dennis's face and said, "Thank you. I know you're telling me the truth." He let go of the other's hand and returned to Michael's side.

Dennis let out a relieved breath. Nick laughed and punched him in the arm. "That was like, eloquent, man. Brought a tear to my eye. Didn't know you had it in you."

Dennis growled. "Shut up, Pinky."

"No, really, Brain. You should write poetry or some shit. Hey, Kaden, you sure part of your power isn't bringing intelligence to idiots? 'Cause I gotta say—"

Dennis turned to Michael and said, "Alpha, Kaden, please excuse me for a moment."

Nick had stopped in mid-sentence when he saw the look that promised death cross Dennis's face, at odds with his polite words, and grinned before taking off at full speed around the side of the house. Dennis was on his heels within seconds and sounds of fighting could be heard just before Missy came out to join them.

"You kids have five minutes to pull your heads out of each other's asses. I expect you to be at the ranch by the time we get there," Michael sent to his Betas.

"Are they at it again?" Joseph asked.

Michael sent the mental equivalent of a laugh. *"Aren't you glad you're on surveillance detail?"* He heard his most mature Beta by far grumbling in his mind and he laughed out loud as he jumped into the driver's side and made sure both Kaden and Missy were buckled in.

As he started the truck and headed out towards the road, he caught the worried look on his mate's face. "Don't worry. Those two are always at it. Dennis is the genius and Nick has all the charm, hence the Pinky and the Brain references. You get used to it." Kaden sent him a doubtful look but he just grinned.

The drive to the ranch was filled with Missy's bubbling personality as she went over some of her courses and explained, in excruciating detail, every minute of the time she'd been spending with Katherine. He didn't mind the constant talking, or even the endless questions, but he'd have to have a talk with his mother about her recent habit of blurting out his more embarrassing moments in life.

As they drew closer, Michael could see Kaden start to fidget as though he was nervous. He reached over and squeezed his mate's hand, confirming his suspicion. He had no idea what Henry must think of Kaden's absence, but the older man was reasonable and he was sure they could work something out for his mate to keep his job and still stay with Michael.

It didn't surprise him that Dennis and Nick were already there, leaning against Dennis's car as they waited. He parked next to them, noticed the state of their clothes, and sighed. Kaden's eyes were huge as he got out of the truck and took in the streaks of dirt and Dennis's busted lip. Nick winked at him and grinned, while the other man grumbled under his breath. Kaden sent a questioning look at Michael, who just shrugged and came around from the other side of the truck to take his hand.

Missy had already jumped out and was bounding up the steps and banging on the door like her life depended on it.

"Do you know where Henry should be around this time?" Michael asked.

Kaden thought for a moment then said, "He's usually in his office. I think his wife was supposed to visit with her family but she should be back by now. She should know where he is." Michael nodded and they both joined Missy on the porch while Nick and Dennis followed a short distance behind.

He couldn't detect any other sounds on the ranch except for those of the animals. Hopefully that meant that all of the workers were elsewhere at the moment. He inhaled deeply and scanned the area, trying to sense anything out of the ordinary. He'd memorised the scents of the murderers the night he had found Kaden in the barn along with Stephen's corpse, but he couldn't smell them now.

"Joseph?"

"All good out here boss. There're a few humans working in the stables but no wolves."

"Keep an eye out. We shouldn't be here for more than an hour or two."

The house was huge, and with no doorbell or intercom system, it could take a while for someone to respond. After a few minutes, though, Henry's wife answered the door. She was a sturdy, middle-aged woman in full cowgirl regalia, including the hat and tassels. Michael recognised her immediately, although he'd only met her once. As soon as she spotted Kaden and his sister, she broke out into a smile that looked like it carried more relief than joy.

"Jade, Missy!" she exclaimed. "I'm so glad to see you two." She instantly wrapped the girl in a strong embrace but, after taking a single step towards Kaden, she seemed to rethink doing the same with him. Michael didn't think it likely that Kaden had made her aware of his power, which told him that Kaden must have a relationship with the Connel's that went beyond employer-employee.

"I was afraid after that incident you'd decided to quit. Henry told me all about it. That man was causing trouble before then and I told Henry we should have fired him months ago but we never thought he would go that far. Are you okay, sweetie?"

Michael saw a faint blush creep into Kaden's cheeks as he answered the woman, but Michael was too busy taking in this new information to pay much attention to their greetings. This was the second time someone had mentioned the fact that his mate had been in danger on the ranch before he'd found him. *And why was she calling him Jade?*

Michael heard his name spoken, pulling him from his thoughts, and looked over at the woman who had addressed him.

"Michael Rockheim, right?" She glanced down at his hand that still held Kaden's but didn't remark on it as she continued, "Cheryl Connel. I think we only met the once at a horse show about a year ago, but my husband raves all the time about your brilliant business mind. Seems you've helped him out on more than a few ventures. It's nice to see you again. Please, come on in." Michael gave her his most charming smile, then glanced back at his Betas.

"This is Nick and Dennis. If you don't mind, they wanted to take a look around the area. It's a beautiful piece of land you've got here. Dennis is thinking about purchasing a few acres of his own, so I thought I'd bring him along so he could get an idea of what exactly he's looking for." It was a small lie, but he needed the men outside to keep an eye on the house while Joseph stayed closer to the barn and the outskirts.

"Not at all. You gentlemen have a quick look-see while I take them to Henry." She turned back to Kaden. "He'll be so happy to see that you're okay. He's been worried about you." Both men nodded and thanked her before Michael turned to close the door. They followed the woman through a spacious living and dining room, then down a long hallway before stopping at a partially open door.

"Henry," she called out as she opened the door to a rustic-looking office. Almost everything inside was made of wood, including the walls, and a few trophy heads of elk and deer adorned the walls. Henry sat behind a huge, oak desk littered with papers, and looked up at the sound of Cheryl's voice. His eyes lit up brightly as he took in their presence, but just as his wife had done, he ignored Michael in favour of Kaden.

"Damn, it's good to see you boy." Henry raised himself from his desk chair and started towards Kaden but seemed to remember himself before he got halfway across the room. There was no doubt in Michael's mind now that Kaden had given them the impression that he didn't like to be touched. He could also see that Henry cared just as much for the man as his wife did.

The older man beamed a smile at Missy, who was ploughing into him almost before he could open his arms to return her hug.

The girl was too excited to slow down, though, and she whirled back to Cheryl, asking, "Has someone been watering my plants? I left a note. I'm sorry I had to leave. Is my garden okay?"

Cheryl, obviously accustomed to the girl's eccentricity, took her by the shoulders and steered her towards the door. "Everything should be fine. Why don't we leave these gentlemen to their business and go check up on your plants?" She closed the door on their way out, giving them a little privacy.

"Hi, Mr Connel. I'm sorry I've been gone for so long. Things have been a little…well…" Kaden's voice lowered and he sent a desperate glance at Michael.

"Son, is this about what happened with Jim?" Henry cast a furtive look at Michael then returned to Kaden. "Did he hurt you again? I called the cops and gave them a report the day you went missing. I didn't give them all the details, but you've never missed a day of work since I hired you and I got worried."

Michael watched Kaden blush furiously again and shake his head. "No, it's nothing like that. I had some other problems I needed to take care of. I'm sorry if I've caused you any trouble."

Henry narrowed his eyes at Kaden as though trying to ascertain whether he was being told the truth or not. Finally, the man turned to Michael and said, "Mr Rockheim, it's good to see you again." He also took notice of their joined hands but ignored it just as his wife had.

Michael had been prepared to deal with the usual rudeness he'd seen other gay couples subjected to and had decided he'd much rather live with that instead of having to let go of his mate for the sake of propriety. Henry surprised him, though, with his air of nonchalance at the occurrence. Michael reached out his other hand and Henry grasped it in a firm handshake before returning to his desk chair.

"I just want you to know, Mr Rockheim, that I don't put up with that sort of behaviour around here. I fired the man as soon as I saw to it that Jade was taken care of. He's a valuable asset to my ranch and I won't have anyone jeopardising his or anyone else's safety while in my employment," Henry said.

Michael looked over at Kaden but his mate kept his head bowed, not willing to meet his eyes. Although he had no idea what Henry was referring to, he could feel his anger rising at the picture the man was painting.

"I know that, Henry, and please, call me Michael. I have a feeling that if you'll still allow Jade to continue to work for you, we'll be seeing a lot more of each other. There is a situation, however, that I need to continue to take care of with Jade. It shouldn't take more than another week at most to resolve. Would you mind terribly if I returned him to you afterward?"

"Not at all," Henry said as he leant back in his chair. "Considering the thousands you've helped me save in financial concerns over the years, I think I can suffer without one of my best workers for a bit longer. That is if that's okay with you, Jade?" Henry turned to the other man with a questioning look.

Kaden finally looked up and, with a huge smile, said, "Thank you, Mr Connel. I'd really appreciate that."

Henry slapped his hand down on the desk and smiled widely. "It's settled then. You got time to visit with Mockingbird before you go? Jake's been working with her but she sure does miss you."

Michael watched the smile on his mate's face widen even more as he nodded vigorously. He had so many questions at this point, he didn't know where to begin, but they would have to wait until tomorrow. He'd promised himself that he'd give his mate at least one day that was carefree, now he just had to bite his tongue long enough to follow through.

Henry walked them out and led the way to the barn where Mockingbird was stabled. By the time Kaden had her saddled and bridled, both he and the horse were practically prancing with excitement. The glow on Kaden's face made him look like a kid in a candy shop, and it got easier and easier for Michael to stave off his questions and suspicions for the day.

While walking the mare to the paddock, both Kaden and Henry filled him in on the progress Kaden had made with the mare. He hated the fact that he needed to relinquish contact with his mate and even grew a little jealous of the horse, but his respect for the young man and the way he put his power to use grew exponentially.

Apparently, Mockingbird had been wild when she was captured by her first owner. After the man had tried unsuccessfully to tame her, he'd started to abuse her when he realised she wouldn't be the money-maker he'd envisioned. When Henry had purchased the mare, his highest hopes had been only to tame her enough to allow him to breed her. Kaden's care and training, however, had resulted in such great strides that Henry was now planning to enter her in show and jumping contests as early as next year.

"There're still a few kinks to work out. She still gets spooked by sudden movements and shadows if she doesn't have an experienced rider on her," Henry was telling him, "but that boy can work wonders I ain't never seen in a horse whisperer."

Michael stood beside the man against the gate surrounding the paddock and they both watched as Kaden put the mare through her paces. The horse seemed just as eager to please him as he was to spend time with her. Michael was struck again by just how lucky he was to have this young man as a mate.

"*Boss,*" Nick sent.

"*What is it?*" Michael immediately went on alert, but kept a part of his attention on Henry, who was still talking to him.

"*One of the stable hands has been watching you and Kaden for the past five minutes. He's human, but the guy just creeps me the fuck out.*"

Michael thought back to the trouble the Connel's had alluded to involving Kaden just before he'd found him again. Henry had sworn that he'd got rid of the troublemaker, but he didn't want to take any chances.

"Keep watching him. Kaden was involved in an altercation with a human here before he witnessed the murder in the barn. Let me know if the man does anything else besides give you the 'creeps'."

Michael could feel the mental equivalent of a growl from Nick as soon as he mentioned the fact that Kaden had been in danger before the murder. He smiled inwardly, pleased that his Betas were willing to protect his mate as much as he was. He'd never thought of himself as particularly lucky in life, but thinking about the strength of his mate, the acceptance of his parents, and the loyalties of his men definitely made him feel like one lucky son-of-a-bitch.

Michael waited until Henry ended the story he was relating to him about how he had met 'Jade', then said, "Henry, I need you to do me a favour," while keeping his eyes on his boy.

Henry shot him a worried look. "Is it concerning Jade here?"

"Yeah."

"Then name it."

Michael sent a brief smile to the man. "I'm worried that there might be the possibility of a threat to Jade. It's through no fault of his own, and it doesn't involve his earlier altercation with one of your workers. I will get to the bottom of it as quickly as possible, but I need to take all the necessary precautions."

"Such as making him take a vacation from work?" Henry asked. When Michael nodded, Henry paused to think for a moment then said, "I like you, Michael. You've never steered me wrong. And I can tell that you and my boy here have some type of relationship going." Michael had to grit his teeth against his conflicting emotions at that statement. On the one hand, he was grateful that Henry could accept their homosexual relationship, but on the other, his instincts screamed at him to tell the man that Kaden was *his* boy, not Henry's or anyone else's. "But I gotta say, you hurt that kid and I'll take it out of your hide."

That comment suddenly dispelled his anger. His mate certainly had a way of endearing himself to people, and he couldn't hold it against Henry for feeling protective over him. "Point well taken," he said with a grin.

"Good, now tell me what you need me to do," Henry said gruffly.

"If anyone asks about Jade or comes by here wanting to speak with him, please call me. You still have my phone number?"

Henry nodded and said, "Will do."

They stood and watched over the next hour as Kaden showed off the little tricks he'd taught to Mockingbird and the improvements she'd made while under his care, commenting here and there whenever the man surprised them with his expertise.

Michael knew Kaden was using his power to communicate with her, but it was still amazing to see the amount of trust the animal had in him. Dennis and Nick joined them eventually to enjoy the show, but Michael could tell they still kept half of their attention on their surroundings.

A little while later, Kaden brought Mockingbird back to the stables where he stripped her of saddle and harness, then rubbed her down affectionately, all the while talking to her soothingly.

Henry bid his farewells and clapped Kaden on the back while shaking his hand. Michael saw his mate's face pale and realised the man must have hit one of the bruises still colouring his back. An irrational surge of anger at the man's ignorant gesture rolled through him, and he had to force himself to stay calm in the face of Kaden's pain. Kaden smiled through it all, though, and he felt his pride in his mate grow even more.

Chapter Eight

By the time they had collected Missy and loaded themselves back into Michael's truck, he couldn't keep his urges in any longer. He pulled Kaden into his arms to give him a gentle but firm hug.

"You're amazing, you know that? The way you use your power. Your patience and dedication. Mother Earth could not have given me a more precious gift than you." Michael squeezed him to emphasise his words, then pulled back to look at the most beautiful face he'd ever seen.

Kaden's cheeks were flushed and his eyes were dancing with delight. The excited animation on his face was breathtaking, and it filled the air with vibrancy.

Michael let Stephen know that they were leaving and made sure that Dennis and Nick were ready to follow them before starting the trip back to his house.

Missy had brought along a few of her flowering plants and some of her more frivolous possessions such as the MP3 player currently blasting her favourite songs through the headphones plugged into her ears. She'd also collected a few of her cookbooks and was content to flip through them in the back seat.

After several minutes of silence, he heard his mate's timid voice ask, "You're not mad at me?"

Michael looked over at him in confusion. "Why would I be mad?"

Kaden swept his eyelids down and stared at his hands folded in his lap, replying, "I know you got angry when you heard Henry call me Jade and mention that...well...that something had happened."

Michael took in the way his mate was wringing his hands and biting his bottom lip in nervousness. It suddenly became imperative that he calm the man's fears, especially due to the fact that they revolved around his reaction to things that he had been unaware of.

"Pulling over, guys. We need a minute." He pulled his truck to the side of the road, which was thankfully free of traffic at this time of day, and unbuckled his seatbelt to turn and give Kaden his full attention. He reached over to grasp one of his hands and instantly felt the increasing amount of anxiety the man was feeling.

"Kaden, I was angry, but only because I'm concerned about you. I don't understand why you felt the need to change your name or why you kept whatever must have happened out there on the ranch from me, but I trust that you have your reasons." Michael reached over with his other hand and unbuckled Kaden's seatbelt as he was talking.

"You've given me no reason to doubt you in the entire time we've been getting to know each other, while I, on the other hand, have given you plenty of reasons to doubt me." He pulled Kaden over to the middle seat beside him and wrapped the smaller man in his arms.

"I know you don't completely trust me yet, and I can't fault you for keeping some things from me, but as long as you let me, I'll be working to rectify that. You're a very talented, charitable, impressive young man, and I hope one day you'll be able to see what I and everyone else sees in you. Until then, please don't be worried when I get angry. It's nothing against you, and in case you haven't noticed, it happens to be part of my charm."

Kaden let out a bark of laughter at that and actually reached his arms around him to hug him back. He could not have hoped for a better response. They held each other for a few minutes before he released his boy and buckled him into the middle seat.

"I want you as close to me as I can get you for the rest of the night," he explained off-handedly. He kept one arm wrapped around his mate and drove the truck back onto the road with the other. He could still feel the heat from the sun in Kaden's platinum hair as his head rested on Michael's shoulder. He couldn't bring himself to lift his jaw from those silken strands for the rest of the trip home.

* * * *

Jim stared at the golden liquid filling his sixth shot glass of the night, although his thoughts were elsewhere. The call he'd just received from his friend still working out on Henry's ranch had taken his mood from happy to downright, disgustingly ecstatic.

The little slut that had got him fired had deserved what had been coming to him. The boy had the body of a sixteen-year-old girl, and flaunted it by running around in tight jeans and shirts that showed off his figure like a damned drama queen, and yet Jim was the one being punished for it.

You dress like a whore, you should expect to be treated like one. Henry, in his old age, was just too damned blind to see that.

He downed the shot and waved the bartender over for a refill.

"I think you've had enough, man. Why don't you call it a night? I can have a cab here in five minutes to take you home."

Jim was about to rip into him when a smooth, deep voice from behind him said, "I'll buy the next one and make sure he gets home all right."

He watched as a twenty was placed on the bar and slid towards the bartender. The man behind the counter shrugged, took the money, then went off to fill the order.

Jim turned in his seat and felt his eyes bulge at the mass of the man behind him. He had to be around six feet with a chest at least half as wide. He raked his gaze down the man's body and took in the expensive threads and posture that spoke of a privileged lifestyle. As much as he despised the look of the stranger, though, he was not about to turn down a free drink.

Jim swivelled his stool back to the bar and grabbed the shot the bartender placed in front of him. Taking it in one swig, he turned back to the large man who was now seated to his left.

"Is there something I can help you with?"

The tall blond looked him over and curled his lip in disgust. "Yes, I'm afraid there is. Do you know a boy named Kaden? Twenty-two, white-blond hair, five-foot-six, a hundred and fifteen, maybe a hundred and twenty-five pounds? Pretty boy?"

Jim snorted. "No, but I know a little bitch goes by that description on the ranch I used to work at."

"And his name would be?"

Jim narrowed his eyes at the stranger. He didn't trust him farther than he could throw him, judging by his aristocratic looks, but he was far too drunk and much too pissed off to care.

"Jade. Name would be Jade. Little slut got me fired. What's it to you?"

A smile that never quite reached the man's eyes slithered across his face and he seemed to glow with interest. "It's what's in it for you that you should be concerned about. I'm prepared to offer you a tidy sum for information on the whereabouts of this boy, as well as your promise of confidentiality. You see, I can't have you running around telling people about our meeting. I hope you understand."

"Are you threatening me?" Jim asked, hearing the slight slur in his own voice.

"Only if I have to," the blond replied. "However, I'd really rather not have to 'threaten you', as you put it. This meeting can be mutually beneficial." The large man reached into his pants pocket and removed a thick bundle of cash wrapped in a rubber band and placed it on the bar between them.

Jim felt excitement flood through him as he eyed the substantial amount of money, but he wanted more than just financial gain. The slut had humiliated him in front of his boss and co-workers, and while he didn't exactly give a shit about what they thought, it was the principle of the matter. The boy had to pay.

"I know where he is, or rather who he's staying with. A friend of mine was gracious enough to fill me in on who he ran off with, but I want my own piece of him. That slut cost me my job and my reputation, and I wanna make sure he pays for it."

Thomas regarded the pathetic human with all the contempt he was due, but kept his comments to himself. This was the best lead they had on the boy and he didn't want to blow their only chance at getting the whore back.

"Done," he lied.

* * * *

"Michael!"

The shout arrested him as he was reaching for the towel on the rack beside the shower and filled his heart with terror. He immediately wrenched open the shower curtain and raced out of the bathroom to see his mate sitting up in his bed, eyes clenched shut and body drenched with sweat.

He jumped onto the bed and encircled him with as much of his body as he could get around him. Kaden was trembling fiercely, still calling out his name, lost in whatever nightmare had a hold on him. Michael tried to still his pounding heart while pouring as much love and soothing emotion as he could manage into the vibrating frame.

Kaden's response was almost immediate, which helped to calm his own fears, but he was still shaking uncontrollably in his arms as Michael lowered him back onto the bed.

"Shhh, baby. I'm here. I'm right here. I won't let you go." He repeated these words over and over again until Kaden slowed his breathing from its sobbing, frantic pace to one that allowed Michael to finally breathe through his own fear. He heard his bedroom door being thrown open and looked over at his father's panicked face.

He continued to soothe the man, who was still asleep but fighting the remnants of his nightmare, as he shook his head, letting the older man know there was no real threat to his mate. Katherine thrust her head inside the door before his father could close it, with a look on her face that said she was ready to tear apart anyone posing as a threat to him or his mate.

He felt a surge of comfort at his mom's love and dedication to Kaden, but the swamping feelings of fear and pain flowing from his mate's body quickly took back his attention.

He lay there for countless minutes after hearing his parents leave, trying to soothe his mate in any way that he could. Eventually, the man gave one last shuddering sigh and drifted back into a fitful slumber. Still Michael couldn't bring himself to release him.

This was definitely not a good way to start out the day when he would be forcing his mate to tell them about the murder he had witnessed, but he knew he couldn't put it off any longer. He wasn't sure how much time had passed before he heard a soft knock on the door. A glance down at Kaden's face showed that the man was still fast asleep, albeit significantly more peacefully, and he slid quietly from the bed.

Outside the door to his room, he found two trays on the floor full of breakfast foods, coffee and orange juice. He smiled at the thoughtfulness of Katherine and Missy, knowing the teen had had a hand in it, and picked them up. Placing them on the dresser, he sat himself gently on the side of the bed next to Kaden.

He started stroking the platinum strands of hair, which shone in the morning rays of the sun streaming through the bedroom window, away from his face. Kaden seemed so at peace right then that he was reluctant to wake him, but they had business to take care of soon that couldn't be delayed any longer.

"I love you, baby," he whispered. The declaration shocked him no less than the first time he'd said it, and it was frightening and welcome at the same time.

"I think I love you, too," Kaden whispered. Michael watched in wonder as pale lids fluttered open and violet eyes pierced him with their intensity. He could feel Kaden's sincerity beaming at him like the shining rays of the sun that lit his hair on fire every time the young man stepped outside. There was an underlying uncertainty to his emotions that let him know his mate was searching for his approval.

He gathered his precious boy into his arms and held him there, rocking him, overcome with happiness and gratitude. He wanted to live in this moment forever. To wrap this strong yet fragile male in his embrace and hide him from the tragedies of his past.

But all too soon the reality of what the day entailed broke into his consciousness and he was forced to pull back from his brief respite and acknowledge their responsibilities. But first...

"I meant it. I do love you. I love everything about you. You're so much more than I ever hoped for in a mate, cock, balls, talent and all." Kaden let loose a peal of laughter that reached into Michael and set his heart to pounding. "You don't have to love me back. I know I still need to earn your trust, but I will…"

"Shhh," Kaden breathed. "I know that I have to tell you about my past today. I can feel your trepidation. I also know that you won't think of me in the same way after I tell you, but for now…right now…I can feel you. All of you."

Kaden's face crumpled in pain, his throat swallowing convulsively, but it wasn't like the pain he had felt from his mate before. It was full of the same kind of yearning he had felt over that interminable length of years he had spent searching for him. Michael reached to pull his mate into his arms again but was stopped by a small but firm hand on his chest.

"I just want you to know that I don't hate you anymore for rejecting me. I know that what happened afterwards was not your fault, and I want you to know that I've always wanted you."

Michael frowned at the cryptic words but Kaden rushed on to say, "I love you. And no matter what happens, I know you're a good man, and I won't blame you for anything you do after today." Michael's frown turned to a full-on black scowl and he was about to argue, but his mate seemed to possess more power than him with the simple, sweet sound of his voice. Kaden stopped him again by distracting him. "So you brought coffee for me?"

He found he could do nothing other than smile and go to the dresser to retrieve the forgotten trays of food. "Actually, we'll have to thank mom and Missy later for this."

"It must be nice having your parents live here with you."

Michael reached over to tuck a lock of blond hair behind Kaden's ear. "They're just staying here to help out for a bit. Dad has more experience with the powers of mages than I do, and I didn't want to end up driving you away with my mistakes." He frowned. "Although that didn't work out quite as well as I thought."

Kaden shrugged. "I think you're doing okay. You should have seen the first time I learnt about my power. It was also the first time I kissed a boy." Kaden's giggle had Michael completely intrigued.

"Well?"

Kaden's cheeks flushed and his lips curved up into the cutest shy smile as he started talking in between stuffing bits of toast into his mouth. "I was with Rayne during lunch recess and we were hiding behind a huge yellow tractor they had in the playground. He was nice to me. I didn't have many friends. Anyways, we kissed, and I thought it was the most wonderful thing in the world. Well, apparently, he did too. When we stopped and left our hiding place, about fifteen other kids close to us were kissing as well." Kaden chuckled down at his food.

"Boys with boys, girls with girls, boys with girls, it didn't matter. It caused a huge fuss and when I told my mom about it that night, she decided to place me in home-schooling. Still, it made me happy to know that I made the first boy I kissed feel so good that his emotions made so many other kids feel good."

He was amazed that Kaden could retain something good from an experience that obviously must have caused him a lot of pain and loneliness afterwards. He remembered when Nick had discovered he was gay at a young age. Michael and Joseph had got into a lot of fights with anyone who would dare insult their friend until Nick was strong enough to defend himself.

Even then, Michael and Joseph – and Dennis by that time – wouldn't tolerate a single rude comment any of the other kids might make about Nick. He could not imagine how hard it must have been for Kaden to deal with not only his newfound power, but also the subsequent isolation.

He tucked two fingers under Kaden's chin and lifted it until he could see those captivating eyes again. "You never cease to amaze me, baby." Kaden smiled shyly and returned to his food. Then Michael had a thought. "Wait, I have to know. Are my kisses as good as your first? 'Cause I've got to admit, I think I'm a little jealous," he grumbled.

Kaden laughed and replied, "Not even close. Your kisses blow his away." Michael wasn't sure if that was true, but it was definitely a boost to his ego. They finished the rest of their breakfast in companionable silence, and he was glad to see that his boy had almost cleared his entire plate. He decided he couldn't put off the inevitable any longer.

They showered together, washing each other's bodies, and even though they were both hard within seconds of stripping off their clothes, neither attempted to push things further. It was enough to simply enjoy each other's presence.

Kaden chose to dress in a pair of jeans and a T-shirt that had belonged to Michael in his teen years, wanting to surround himself with the faint, lingering aroma of his mate on the clothes. After following Michael out of the room and downstairs, they washed their dishes in the sink without speaking. In fact, Kaden noticed that the entire house was eerily quiet.

When he asked where Missy was, Michael informed him that she and Katherine had taken the day to go shopping. Knowing his sister, that could be an all-day event, especially if there was a chance she could get out of her studies.

When they were done, Michael turned and pulled him into a fierce embrace. Kaden knew that he should be distancing himself from the man to prepare for what he was sure would be the last time his mate would want to touch him, but couldn't bring himself to give up this precious moment. Grief over his impending loss threatened to surge up and drown him, but he fought it down, not wanting it to ruin what little time he had left.

When Michael pulled away to give him a reassuring smile, he felt his face reflect the man's expression and allowed Michael to lead him through the living room and down the hall.

His office was spacious but already filled with the company of Sam and Michael's Betas. Nick and Dennis stood in front of several bookshelves that were stacked from floor to ceiling and took up most of one wall. Joseph stood at the opposite wall, leaning against a filing cabinet, and Sam sat in a recliner to the side of Michael's desk.

Michael took Kaden to the loveseat resting against the far wall across from the door and sat him down. Kaden expected him to take a seat next to him but the man gave him a tender kiss on the forehead then continued to his desk chair, where he sat down stiffly.

Kaden felt suddenly very vulnerable and started to pick at a hole in the knee of the jeans, keeping his gaze on his lap. The silence was so ominous that Kaden almost jumped when the deep, resonant voice of his mate broke the stillness.

"Okay, baby. We'll try to make this as short as possible. Because of your power, I need you to tell us everything you know without anyone touching you so that we know you're not being influenced by another's emotions."

Kaden supposed that sounded like a valid reason, but all he could think about was how bereft he felt without the solid feel of his mate beside him, touching him.

"Why don't you start with who the killers are?"

Kaden took a breath and let it out slowly between his teeth. He could do this. It was the right thing to do, even if it did put him in danger. Even if he would have to run again.

He repeated that to himself as he answered, "Thomas, Brook and Daniel." He looked up at Michael, but knew by the sober expression on the man's face that he would need to do this on his own. "They're Alpha Gregory's Betas. Their clan is located here in Missouri, up north."

"Sorry, but if I can interrupt for a moment, that doesn't make any sense," Dennis spoke up. "All three of us," he made a broad gesture to include himself, Joseph and Nick, "searched Stephen's place and found several contact numbers belonging to guys I did background checks on and they were all located out of state, and most of them were human. I was also able to look up his bank statements over the past few years and found that he was receiving funds from many different domestic accounts, though I wasn't able to identify who those accounts belonged to.

"From what I gathered, Stephen was trading goods for several different people of influence. Are you saying that an Alpha put a hit on a wolf dealing with humans? If that's the case, we could be dealing with something that's a little more serious than just a clan issue."

Kaden felt his hopes of keeping the information he had to a bare minimum vanish as he listened to Dennis' words. While he appreciated the fact that the man was smart enough to figure all of that out without any outside help, he also cursed him for it. He could feel the overwhelming sense of despair and pain grow in his chest and felt a single tear escape as he looked up at Michael and tried to memorise the features of the only man he had ever loved.

He gave himself only seconds, though, before falling into the headspace he always retreated to when he was forced to deal with something he knew he couldn't handle. It settled over him like a familiar cloak and he took comfort in the emptiness he found there.

Nothing could touch him here. There were no emotions, no dreams, no pain.

Kaden stood and walked to the window behind the loveseat, staring unseeingly out at the expanse of grass and trees, and started from the beginning.

"After I discovered my power, I tried to keep people from touching me, which was easy for a while, but I had to get a job. It took me a bit, but eventually I learnt to harness the emotions of others and keep them inside me, so that when I...when I sold myself, I wouldn't project the emotions of whoever was touching me too far. It didn't always work, especially if the emotions were powerful."

Kaden shivered as he remembered the night this had all come about. "When I saw Michael, I was drawn to him. I felt like I could finally know what a home was if I just made him notice me, but...well...Alpha Gregory saw him reject me. He knew that if an Alpha was rejecting me, then I must be clanless, and somehow he knew I was part mage. He took me behind the building and he..." Kaden choked back a pained cry and worked to find his headspace again. "He took me back to his place after that and discovered what my power was because I couldn't contain it. He was so strong, so demanding. I couldn't keep his emotions inside me.

"Gregory and his Betas started to take me with them to people who they wanted to influence. Powerful people. Gregory would touch me and project his feelings onto them, convincing them to give him money, sign deals, offer lands that he would turn around and sell at a profit." Kaden felt his voice fading and cleared his throat. He had to get through this, and he could, as long as he kept his gaze focussed on the scenery outside the window he was facing. As long as he didn't catch the look of disgust he was sure was on Michael's face.

"He also used me to kill someone once, just to see if he could. I was a conduit, and the emotions he poured into me crippled the man. He never stood a chance." Kaden paused to take a shuddering breath. "I never met this Stephen, but if Gregory sent his Betas to kill him, he had to have been in Gregory's employ."

Kaden stopped, not knowing what else to add, and a thick cloud of silence descended upon all those in the room with him. It was eerie and almost suffocating, but he was reluctant to say any more than he absolutely had to. He stayed lost in his headspace, hoping that if he ignored the rest of the story, everyone else would as well.

Of course, his luck always went from bad to worse.

"Did you try to stop him? Tell anyone what was going on?" Nick asked.

A wrenching sob tore through Kaden's chest before he could stop it. He felt his stomach heave and try to rid itself of its contents as he tried desperately to regain control. He wrapped his arms around his waist in an attempt to hold himself together, and hunched his shoulders. Alone and sick to the very depths of his soul, he paused for several minutes until he managed to find that emptiness that surrounded him with familiarity, as if welcoming him home.

In a deadpan voice, he replied, "No. I'm sorry." He turned to look into the eyes of every man in the room, knowing they probably wouldn't believe him, and also knowing that he was saying goodbye. "Between the beatings and the starvation that lasted for days on end, being locked in a cage and used daily as a whore and a power source for him and his Betas, no." Anger rose within him and the humiliation of what he'd been forced to suffer for years suddenly came to be too much.

"No!" he yelled. "No!" Tears flowed freely down his cheeks and his body trembled so much he thought he might shatter from the force.

He looked straight at Michael and cried, "He broke me. Every day they broke me." He swung his glare to Nick. "And before you ask, the answer is no, I didn't try to fight him as a wolf. My mom ran with us after my father was killed and we had to hide from all mages and weres to avoid the same fate. I had no one to teach me to shift, so I couldn't fight them in were-form because that obviously didn't happen."

He immediately regretted the insult to Michael, but couldn't bring himself to care anymore about how he sounded. The horror he saw on each and every one of their faces was enough. It was done. He'd played his part, and he wasn't going for sainthood here, so it was time to leave. He would collect Missy tonight, but for now, he had to get out.

He walked to the office door and left the room as if on auto-pilot. Each step he took towards the front door of the house was made in silence, and each tear that fell at the absence of the sound of his mate running to stop him was like a knife tearing at his soul. It ripped the tattered, pathetic pieces left over from years ago until there was nothing left.

His body paused as his hand reached for the front doorknob. He absolutely hated that incessant voice at the back of his mind that told him to wait. That maybe, if he held off for just a bit longer, Michael would come for him, but it was the same hope he had held onto for the past four years, and it was time to let it go.

Kaden scrubbed at his eyes and yanked the door open but managed to stop himself just before he childishly slammed it closed. The glare of the afternoon sun dazed him, causing more tears to blur his sight as he stumbled down the front porch and across the driveway. Before he could wipe them away, though, something solid and sharp struck the back of his skull and the blinding brightness of the sun was all he saw before the world went black.

Michael watched as his mate opened and closed the door to his office, leaving a room full of shocked men in his wake. He wanted to go after him, to force him to stay while Michael's mind caught up to the implications of the man's testimony, but he couldn't risk touching him in the state he was in.

He had never before felt such all-consuming, unadulterated rage as he felt at that moment. Anger at himself for leaving his mate to be subjected to the horror he'd had to live through for years. Anger at Kaden's mother for not providing for her son the way she should have, but especially anger at that son-of-a-bitch, at all those bastards, who had hurt Kaden.

Sam's voice eventually broke through the roaring in his ears. "Michael, I can't pretend to know what you're feeling right now, but I think we need to come up with a plan, and soon. I doubt that the rest of Alpha Gregory's clan knows what he's been up to and we can't afford any more deaths."

Michael focussed on his father's words enough to let the haze of red that clouded his vision fade. Taking in the concerned faces of the men standing in the room with him, he saw his own anger mirrored in their eyes. His hands shook slightly as he leaned his head forward and wrenched at his hair, using the pain as a sort of release for the violence swirling around in his head.

The truth had been in front of him the whole time. The scars, the fear of people, the cryptic words here and there. All alluding to what the boy had been through over the past several years.

How could he not have pieced it together before now? How could he have been so blind?

"I should have known. I should have searched for him harder." He looked at his father pleadingly, as if the man might be able to offer him some sort of reason how he could have failed his mate so completely.

If he were being truthful, he would admit that he was also looking for censure in the man's gaze. Here he had been blessed with a life full of people who loved him, who were willing to lay down their lives to protect his honour and safety, and all while his mate had known none of that. Michael had only added to his misery from the moment the pup had silently asked for help when they'd first met.

"Alpha Michael," Joseph said formally. "With all due respect, sir, I think we all owe your mate an apology, but I also think Sam is right. Our self-recriminations should come later. If this Alpha Gregory is behind the murder and has been using Kaden's power for years, we should take the asshole into custody and bring him before a tribunal of our clan as well as his. If what Kaden is saying is true, and I don't doubt him for a second, then I'm also inclined to agree that this Gregory and his Betas have kept their clan in the dark about their...use...of the young man."

Michael fought to gain control of his roiling emotions and pulled his head from his hands to sit back. "Yes. Of course you're right. Dad, have you ever heard of Gregory or his clan?"

"Only in passing reference," his father said. "From what I know, it seems the man has accrued a considerable amount of wealth over the past several years, although I haven't heard anything about him recently. We should ask Kaden how long ago he managed to get away from Gregory. That will at least give us an idea about when he was using the boy so that we can more accurately track his financial transactions. It could also clue us in as to who he's been doing business with."

"Agreed," Dennis chimed in. "If Gregory is dealing with humans as well as wolves, we need to find out exactly who in order to minimise exposure. As appalling as it is that one of our own would be willing to risk the secret of our existence from humans just to make a buck, it's not the first time it's happened. Hopefully, though, it won't turn into the disaster it caused the last time."

"That time it was a group from a clan up in Washington State, wasn't it?" Nick asked. "I remember that. It didn't end pretty."

Michael nodded and pushed back from his desk, standing up. They were right. The situation warranted their immediate attention, which meant he couldn't afford the luxury of anger right now. He needed to concentrate on the matter at hand.

"All right gentlemen, it looks like we have our work cut out for us. I'll get Kaden back in here to see if he can give us any more information. Meanwhile, Dennis, see if you can find anything on Gregory through the 'net. Dad, if you know anyone that might know something about the man, that would be great. I'll be right back."

Dennis took his seat at the desk to jump on his computer while Michael left the office to find his mate. He went upstairs and searched his room but came up empty. A quick investigation of the bathroom, kitchen, living room and spare rooms also proved to be fruitless.

By the time he got to the back yard, where he inhaled deeply but couldn't find a trace of the man's scent, fear had replaced every lingering ounce of anger and his senses went on full alert. Running back into the house and towards the front door, he yelled, "Kaden!" but there was no reply.

Once in the driveway, he detected the faint scent of ocean spray that belonged to his boy, along with a few other scents that were vaguely familiar. In the few moments it took for his father and Betas to join him outside, his memory kicked in.

The men from the barn. Their scents were blended in with that of his mate, but they went no farther than the front of the house. He ignored his men's questions and concentrated on the ground, spotting the presence of tire tracks that didn't belong to any of their vehicles. The tracks ended where dirt met concrete, as did their combined scents.

They had his mate. The sick bastards had the audacity to snatch him right in front of his home.

Once again, he'd failed his mate out of negligence, and the only one paying for his inability to take proper care of the man was Kaden himself. Only this time, Michael was fully aware of what he'd lost. He knew his mate's sweet, innocent smile, his charming desire to put the needs of others above his own, his bright, contagious laughter.

This time, he knew exactly what the man would suffer due to his failure to protect him, and he had no one to blame but himself. Again.

There was no holding back his black rage. He screamed out his frustration and his men and father had the good sense to vacate his immediate presence as he found the nearest thing to him and threw it with all of his were strength across the lawn. The lawnmower snapped the trunk of a ten year old tree some twenty yards away with a loud crunch.

"Michael!" his father yelled.

"They took him! Sam, they took him while I was sitting inside trying to get over his past. He's living it all over again because I couldn't get my head out of my ass long enough to comfort him. To protect him." He heard his voice crack but he didn't care. His mate was suffering at the hands of monsters and he had done nothing to prevent it.

"Then we get him back, all of us, but you need to focus. Your mate needs you, and we will stop at nothing to help you get him back." The deadly, determined lock in his father's eyes, mirrored in the faces of his Betas, encouraged him to marshal his chaotic thoughts and assume the role he'd been preparing for his entire life. He was their Alpha, his mate's Alpha, and he'd be damned if he was going to let someone else usurp his role.

"We have work to do."

* * * *

Pain erupted in Kaden's skull as he felt a large hand strike the side of his face with a force that snapped his head back, spraining his neck. Another slap had blood bursting from his lips and filling his mouth.

A rough grip yanked the front of his shirt upwards then slammed him back down. He blearily blinked open his eyes to stare into the face that haunted his dreams and filled his waking thoughts with dread. He could feel the sickening emotions of lust, pride, and anticipation course through him, radiating from the man's touch and threatening to drown him in their intensity.

The cold, hard grit of concrete pressed into the flesh of his back and the weight of the powerful man above him made the dank air in the room seem more and more oppressive by the second. He didn't need to look around to know that he was in Gregory's basement. The smell and cold and darkness of the room were as familiar to Kaden as the pain he had come to associate with the man looming over him.

The fear that had consumed every cell of his being for longer than he cared to remember returned in full force. He'd managed to put it aside over the past year for Missy's sake. Learnt to bury it so that he could have the chance to explore a world that didn't revolve around pain and humiliation, but it was back. Living and breathing, inside him and on top of him, and he could feel his chest burning in an attempt to suck in air that he couldn't pull into his lungs fast enough.

"Did you really think you could hide from me forever? I own you, boy." Gregory grabbed hold of his hair and wrenched his head painfully to the side. "And I see you've been letting someone else enjoy your body." Gregory leaned his head down and bit viciously into the mating mark left from Michael.

The pain of the man's fangs as he tore into the sensitive skin of his neck was nothing like the untainted, arousing passion that Michael evoked in him. That one act, that one desecration of the only thing in his life that was still pure and beautiful and perfect, was more than he could take. It felt worse than any violation of his body and emotions he had been forced to suffer through by this man.

He twisted his neck away from Gregory's jaws, feeling the tendons in his neck tear and warm blood spurt from the wound to splash onto his chest and spill to the floor beneath him.

Agonising pain swept through him, searing every nerve ending from his abdomen to his scalp, but his act of defiance was well worth it. He'd spent almost his entire life bending to the will of others. Learning to fear the physical pain they subjected him to as well as the emotions they bombarded him with out of their own ignorance or for their personal gain.

Gregory's distant, angry shout would have brought a smile to his lips had he been able to control the muscles in his neck and face, but he could settle for the satisfaction of the man's curses.

"Stupid little whore!" Gregory said between clenched teeth.

Kaden knew the gash and loss of blood wouldn't kill him, but it would force the Alpha to give him time to heal before the man could risk using him in any way. Gregory spat the blood still in his mouth onto Kaden's cheek, cursing him before he brought the back of his hand across his face again, causing Kaden's vision to blur and new pain to blossom in his head.

The door to the basement opened and Kaden could just make out Thomas's scent as he heard the Beta ask, "Is he awake yet? Shit, Gregory, what the hell did you do?"

"Just reclaiming my property. The boy did this to himself," Gregory growled.

Thomas took in all the blood coating Kaden's body and spreading in a puddle on the floor and shook his head. "We need to use his power. Now. Deals are falling through and…"

"We've waited a year and a half—we can wait a few more days. By then, he'll at least be able to sit in with me for a few conferences. We can renew deals with other weres here first, then we'll start visiting with the humans."

Gregory ripped Kaden's shirt from his chest to use as a compress to stanch the flow of blood. When he applied more pressure than needed, Kaden had to bite the inside of his cheek hard enough to draw blood in order to keep from crying out. Between the pain and lethargy from blood loss, it was getting hard for him to follow their conversation.

"Fine, but I don't think you should use him for your own entertainment until then either. The sooner he heals, the sooner we can get things taken care of," Thomas said.

Gregory fisted his other hand in Kaden's hair and dragged him to the back wall of the basement while chuckling. "Oh, I don't think we need to worry about that. It's using his power that saps his energy. Isn't that right, boy?" Kaden managed a weak glare as Gregory placed a steel cuff, on a short chain bolted to the wall, around his ankle.

"Gregory," Thomas growled in warning.

"Whatever. I'll leave him alone. Meanwhile, we have meetings to set up. Get the others and meet me in my office."

Thomas gave one last leering look at Kaden, then turned and left to do his Alpha's bidding. Gregory proceeded to rip his jeans from him roughly and jerked his head towards a rusted pot lying three feet away.

"You know where to do your business. I suggest you use these next few nights to rest up. I'm looking forward to giving you your punishment for running from me." He placed his hand back over the wound in his neck and squeezed until Kaden let out a cry of pain. "And you try to pull any more stunts like this and I'll break your fingers, you understand me, boy?"

The threat wasn't idle, but Kaden couldn't bring himself to respond. Thankfully, Gregory was too impatient to set up his meetings with the men he planned to manipulate using Kaden's power to stay and push the issue. The large Alpha rose from the ground and strode out of the door. Kaden could hear the loud click of the padlock on the other side as Gregory locked him in.

Alone, naked and in pain, Kaden allowed the darkness and familiarity of the room to surround him and swallow his fears like it always did. This is where Gregory always brought him to be punished or to await his punishment.

What the man didn't know was that this room had always offered Kaden a measure of solace and escape when he was left alone. Like any arrogant, conceited prick, Gregory believed that anyone would rather be in his presence than out of it, but down here, Kaden could lose himself in his secret dreams.

Only this time, there were no dreams. No hopes, no desires. No fantasies that his mate would come to his rescue like he had imagined so many times in the past.

He'd walked out on Michael without even waiting for their last week together to end like he had promised he would. There had been no mistaking the looks of anger and disgust on the faces of every man in that office where he had laid bare his past. What's more, he had yelled at Michael again for rejecting him at their first meeting.

He didn't have the energy to blame his mate for the result of his life anymore.

Kaden tried not to let his fears over Missy's future consume him. He was fairly positive that if Katherine didn't take her in, Cheryl would. Katherine would be able to teach her about her were blood and possibly find information to help her with her power.

He wasn't sure if the brief respite from his misery, his job at the ranch and his few days of happiness with Michael, had been worth it or not. It felt as if he had been given a taste of what everyone else took for granted, only to feel more pain as it was ripped away so suddenly.

He wanted to rage against the injustice of it all. To scream and cry and reject the world that had tossed him away before even giving him a chance to live, to love, but it would do no good. He would escape again. He was stronger and wiser than before. There was no doubt that he would be able to find a way, but for now, he would endure like he'd always done.

He began to think of his time at the lake and the lessons Michael had taught him about shifting. As painful as the memory of the man was, remembering those words might be his only chance to escape this time. He had no doubt that Gregory would be watching him more carefully, but being able to shift would definitely help when an opportunity to run made itself available.

Chapter Nine

It had been three days—*three days*—since his mate had been taken from him. The stress of waiting was eating away at Michael's mind and insides like acid. Dennis had pulled up records of Alpha Gregory's bank accounts and influxes of cash that were unaccounted for, but they couldn't accuse the man on that find alone.

No one in Gregory's or Michael's pack knew about Kaden except for his men, parents and Gregory's Betas, so it would be one Alpha's word against the other. With Kaden's questionable background and mage blood, Michael had to admit that the man's testimony might be looked upon as unreliable.

This morning, however, Mother Earth must have decided to reward their efforts to unravel the truth because they finally got the break they needed. Joseph, in his oh-so-charming, threatening way, had managed to intimidate a wolf belonging to Alpha Gregory's clan whom they had discovered was doing business with the man.

Fortunately, it had not been hard to convince Gustin that his Alpha had been taking advantage of him. For years, Gustin had been meeting with Gregory in order to discuss the financial plans and state of his expansive landscaping business. He'd admitted to leaving every meeting feeling confident that his business was producing successful profits, but the numbers never added up when taxes came due and his accounts wouldn't match the sums of his inventory.

Gustin had also admitted to having seen a young man who fitted Kaden's description on occasion, at Gregory's house during his meetings with the man, but had been told he was a relative from another clan. Michael had been appalled to learn of the blatant disregard Gregory obviously had for his clan, but even worse was the fact that his clan members had seemed to accept the sad state of affairs.

They weren't a large community, and when Michael had asked the man if he had ever become suspicious of the fact that their Alpha always seemed to have more money than their clan could produce, he had just shrugged with a guilty look on his face. Michael had never wanted to slap the stupidity out of someone more in his entire life.

They needed him, though, so Michael had reined in his sudden homicidal urges and worked with him, Sam and his Betas to come up with a plan set to be executed that night. Gustin had been called by Thomas, one of Gregory's Betas, a few days ago to meet with his alpha tonight at seven.

The fact that this was his first meeting with his Alpha in almost a year and Kaden had been taken just days ago was too much of a coincidence for Michael. He was positive that Gregory was planning to use Kaden at some point during the meeting.

However, they wouldn't be able to rely on Gustin very much, considering he would probably come under the influence of the Alpha's emotions, broadcast through Kaden, within minutes. That left Gustin with a very small window in which to notify Michael and his Betas via the mic set they'd attached to his chest underneath his shirt. It was a very human, very risky tactic, but also their only means of communication. From the information Gustin had been able to provide to them about Gregory, Michael was sure that the Alpha would be too confident in himself to consider that one of his own might go against him.

Michael looked up from the coffee table in his living room, where he and his men were going over the map of Gregory's territory, to see Sam escorting Gustin in from the kitchen. Two men who had acted as Sam's Betas before his father retired walked in with them, completing their rescue and containment crew. The idea was to incarcerate and convict Gregory and his Betas with as few deaths as possible, but everyone understood that Kaden's safety was top priority.

Michael noticed that Gustin was fidgeting with nervousness. He had only one part to play, but going against one's Alpha, even if it was the right thing to do, was never easy.

"Is everyone set?" Sam, Gustin and Nick nodded.

Once Michael got confirmation from Gustin over his earpiece that Kaden was in the house, he would inform Sam, who would be coming in through the back with his own Betas, through their mental link. Michael would be leading Nick, Joseph and Dennis through the front entrance since, according to Gustin, it was the closest to Gregory's office.

He looked at the man and asked, "You remember what to say if you see the young man there?"

Gustin smiled wanly and said, "Yeah. My daughter is expecting pups. Are you sure you'll be able to get past the alarms on the doors, though?"

"Got it covered," Dennis said from across the room.

Gustin nodded but continued, "Uhh...Alpha Michael?"

Michael knew what was coming. He and his father had discussed every possible outcome for this scenario and there was only one topic that had yet to come up in the group. "Go ahead, Gustin."

"Well...I'm not contesting the fact that my Alpha needs to be held accountable for his actions but, as you're probably already aware, we'll be without an Alpha afterwards. If his Betas are in on his schemes also, well..."

Michael curbed his impatience and replied, "Don't worry. I would never leave a clan to fend for themselves if there was anything I could do about it. I'd be willing to accept your members into my own clan, or help out until you could choose another member fit to be Alpha." Gustin let out a sigh of relief and nodded gratefully.

"Okay then," Michael said. Let's load up. It'll take us a few hours to get there, and I want us to be in position well before the meeting. Gustin, Sam will drop you off at your place so you can go directly from there to Gregory's house."

He didn't tell the man that Sam would also be keeping an eye on him until he left for the meeting. It wouldn't do to lose the key person in this mission because the man suddenly got a case of the nerves.

Michael walked everyone out, waiting until they had climbed into their cars and left before walking to his own truck. A soft hand on his elbow stopped him and he turned to see his mother standing there with a fierce look on her face.

"I don't think I need to tell you that you will have one pissed-off mother if you don't bring both of my sons home safe, right?"

Michael laughed and pulled her into a tight hug. "No, Mom, I figured that was a given. Don't worry. We'll be back before you know it."

Missy was standing a few feet away, hugging herself and looking lost. Her presence had been the hardest part about having to wait these past three days. Her happiness had turned into despondency and she'd taken to quietly following him around every chance she got.

When he'd asked her why she didn't want to spend time with Katherine anymore, she'd said, "I can smell Kaden on you." After that, he had started camping out in the living room with her at night while she slept so she could stay close as much as possible.

He turned to her now and wrapped her tiny body in his arms, then kissed her forehead. "Make sure Mom doesn't eat all of the brownies you made for our return, okay?"

Missy smiled tentatively and Katherine let out an inelegant snort but backed away as he got into his truck. He couldn't help but grin at the woman's tenacity. It had taken Sam an entire day to convince her to stay behind. She would have been right there with them but for the little girl standing next to her.

Heading towards the road, he cleared his mind of everything but the task at hand.

* * * *

Kaden turned off the bathroom light before taking out a washcloth from the side cabinet and soaking it in warm water at the sink. He had no desire to see his reflection or look at his body, and though his vision wasn't as acute as other weres', he had years of practice at cleaning himself up in the dark. His hands were shaking from lack of food and sleep, causing him to spill water onto the floor, but it would hurt too much to take a shower.

Gregory's promise not to punish him until they conducted their necessary meetings hadn't held out.

He blotted the wet cloth gingerly against what skin he could reach. His shoulders still ached too much to allow him to lift or cross his arms to their full extent.

Fortunately, his face was still too smooth to require that he shave, so he wouldn't have to aggravate the bruises on his jaw. He hung the washcloth on the rack beside the cabinet and picked up the bottle of shampoo Gregory always kept for him underneath the sink, along with toothpaste and a toothbrush still in its wrapper. He quickly brushed his teeth, then washed his hair over the side of the tub, not surprised when his hands came away full of thick clumps of it.

He didn't particularly care about what his hair looked like, but he hated it when they constantly thinned it out by yanking roughly on it. It meant that he had less to hide his face behind. After rinsing, he blindly reached out and took the towel from the rack, gently dried his hair, then folded it across the edge of the tub. He stayed in his kneeling position on the floor, though his knees throbbed, and rested his head on the towel with a barely audible sigh.

He was locked inside the bathroom and didn't want to leave the sanctuary of the darkness any sooner than he absolutely had to. Every muscle in his body ached. His skin was on fire from the numerous lashes that had split it open, and his head pounded mercilessly. But none of that could compare to the despair clawing at his chest, threatening to burst out of him in huge sobs.

He'd thought he could get through this until he found a way to escape again, but his will to keep going until then was almost completely gone. How could he have forgotten the sickness of the emotions he was forced to endure as Gregory pounded into him, deepening his assault with every cry that was brutally wrenched from Kaden's lips? The constant battering of hatred and anger and greed took more out of him than any beating ever could.

He was beginning to wish he had never escaped in the first place. Just thinking about that brief amount of freedom and knowing he might never get it back was almost enough to make him lose hope, and he couldn't afford that.

He jerked at the sudden loud banging on the door and heard the lock release before Thomas exposed him to the light in Gregory's bedroom through the doorway.

He couldn't keep himself from flinching away from the man as he reached for him, which only served to piss Thomas off even more. "I may be under orders to get you ready, but Gregory didn't say anything about having to keep my hands from you," Thomas sneered as he grabbed a handful of his hair and dragged him over to the bed. "You take any more time being lazy, and I'll make sure you're in too much pain to sleep tonight."

For emphasis, Thomas grabbed his penis and squeezed until tears slipped from the corners of Kaden's eyes and he let out a soft wail. Kaden knew Gregory had warned his Betas that he was off-limits to them until Gregory was done punishing him, but Gregory's threats had never stopped them before, and it wouldn't stop Thomas now. He knew Kaden wouldn't risk another beating by telling the Alpha.

Kaden would have laughed at the empty threat of Thomas' words if not for the pain. He hadn't slept since they'd brought him here days ago. He doubted that would change tonight. Kaden hissed as Thomas wrenched out even more hair from his head when he released him.

Taking a moment to regain his balance, he began to dress in the outfit that was laid out for him on the side of the bed.

Everything was in black, and even though the material was soft, it still felt like steel wool on his battered body. Gregory didn't like to take the chance of someone noticing the blood that occasionally seeped through the cloth when one of Kaden's wounds opened up during a conference.

They were meeting with a wolf tonight, however, who would be able to smell his blood if he started bleeding and would be likely to get suspicious. It meant that Gregory and his betas would have to treat him a little more gently than usual so as not to reopen a wound until the meeting was concluded.

Lucky me, he thought as he finished getting dressed and rose to retrieve the hairbrush lying on the dresser behind him. He studiously kept his head down and turned away from the mirror before lightly running the brush through his hair, pulling out even more blond strands. At this rate, he could be bald in a week or two.

Gregory had forbidden him to don footwear at any time now as an extra precautionary measure to keep him from running again, so he was led barefoot down two sets of stairs and along a long, dark hallway.

As they entered Gregory's office, where he always conducted his business, Kaden let years of habit take over and mutely took a seat at the end of a long couch against the nearest wall. Gregory had already positioned himself to stand within casual reach of Kaden so that he could be ready to use his emotional influence when necessary.

Kaden never looked up, but he recognised the scent of a clan member from several previous deals, during which Gregory had conned him into giving his Alpha an extremely inflated percentage of his yearly profits.

Not that he cared.

The men Gregory dealt with either ignored him completely or looked at him with lust in their eyes. Gregory's one good quality was that he wasn't into sharing, other than with his Betas. Kaden remembered that this member had always barely noticed his existence, which helped to calm his fears a fraction.

Gregory usually waited to touch Kaden until he started to see doubt cross the faces of the people he was conning, but this time, he immediately reached to place his hand on the back of his neck. Before he was able to make contact, though, his guest blurted out, "So, Alpha Gregory, have I told you yet that my daughter recently discovered that she's to have a litter of pups soon?"

Gregory quickly recovered from that unexpected interruption and continued to settle his hand against Kaden's skin. "Why no, you haven't," he replied smoothly. "I'd love to hear all about it, but perhaps at another time. We have plenty of business to discuss and unfortunately not a lot of time to do it in, wouldn't you agree?"

Kaden didn't have to look into the guest's eyes to see the confidence and devotion that would soon be reflected in his voice. He could feel both emotions being transmitted through him, as well as impatience to take care of their dealings as quickly as possible. He lowered his head even more as he felt his own disgust for himself rise and tried in vain to retreat to that corner of his mind that allowed him to become oblivious to his surroundings.

Thomas acted as courier, transferring necessary paperwork back and forth between the two men, so that Gregory wouldn't be forced to relinquish his hold on Kaden.

Though they managed to take care of business and end their meeting in less than fifteen minutes, which was extremely expedient considering the amount of financial generosity the guest had just unwittingly agreed to, it seemed to Kaden as though hours had gone by. The manipulation of his power against his will always forced him to expend great amounts of energy and left him feeling nauseous.

By the time the meeting was concluded, Kaden felt so depleted that once his head fell to the side of the cushion he was resting against, he couldn't bring himself to raise it again.

Thomas walked the guest to the door of the office where Gregory's other two Betas were waiting to escort him out of the house. Thomas then immediately began to file away the signed paperwork, concluding the coerced deal Gregory had made, while the Alpha removed his hand from Kaden's neck and walked over to his desk to pour himself a glass of brandy.

"I think that went well." He gulped down the contents in one swallow, refilled it, then poured another glass to hand to Thomas. "Have you set up meetings with the other members yet?"

Thomas walked from the filing cabinet to the side of the desk after sealing the combination lock and accepted the proffered glass. "Yes. We have two scheduled for tomorrow night, then a conference with the mayor the day after."

Gregory chuckled and downed his second shot before saying, "Excellent. We'll hit the major figureheads first, then deal with the little guys. That reminds me. We'll need to find a replacement for that idiot, Stephen." He paused to cast a disgusted look at Kaden, no doubt frustrated with his lack of endurance. "Take him to my bedroom. I have a few calls to make, but I'll up shortly."

Kaden closed his eyes and bit his tongue to keep from whimpering in expectation of what was to come, but suddenly, a booming crash sounded from the direction of the front door. Gregory paused in the action of pouring himself another drink to yell at Thomas to find out what was going on.

Thomas was running down the hall before he'd even finished his sentence and Kaden held his breath as Gregory stood still, most likely communicating with his Betas through the mind-link they shared. With a feral growl, the tall man abruptly turned and yanked Kaden from the couch by his arm, starting for the office door.

Kaden was finally able to focus enough to realise that something was wrong when more crashes and the sounds of wolves snarling and howling filled the previously still air. He struggled to keep up with the Alpha but the grip on his arm was causing the gashes across his back to tear open and the pain made him stumble into a floor lamp next to the door.

The hold on him tightened, the only thing keeping him from collapsing to the floor, when the form of a massive black wolf barrelled into the room, hitting Gregory square in the chest. The force of the collision caused the man to fall back into Kaden who subsequently hit the lamp again, but this time with his back.

Pain exploded throughout his body but the scream that erupted from his throat was cut off when his head slammed back onto the floor now beneath him. His vision blurred and it felt as though his eardrums would bleed from the deafening thunder of roars and growls.

Kaden wanted to run and hide, not in the least ashamed of his cowardice at that moment, but just then, the intoxicating aroma of a spring forest and musk hit his senses so hard, it seemed to clear his mind of all other thoughts. Wiping tears of pain from his eyes, he blinked rapidly until he was able to observe the scene before him.

There were two wolves fighting viciously on the other side of the room, one black, the other a russet brown. They appeared to be equally matched in height and girth but their movements were so fast that Kaden was having trouble distinguishing one from the other. There was no doubt in his mind, however, that the black wolf was Michael.

The pair crashed about the room, demolishing the furniture around them, but the majority of the damage to their bodies they caused themselves. Though the evidence that Michael had actually come for him this time was fighting right in front of him, he felt no elation or joy.

Dread and fear for his mate consumed his every thought and feeling as he watched the battle going on before him in horror.

They were too evenly matched.

Claws and fangs and fur all rolled into a blur until he couldn't track one movement to another. The only proof that they were causing each other damage was sprayed across the walls and floor in large, crimson arcs and splatters.

A gasp was wrenched from his throat when one of the wolves was thrown by the scruff of his neck by the other. It hurtled through the air and into a bookcase that lined the wall behind the desk. There was a loud, sickening crack as its massive form slammed into the shelves before falling into a heap on the ground.

Only then was Kaden able to realise that it was his mate lying injured and vulnerable to his enemy. His mate, who didn't get up immediately while the russet-coloured wolf cautiously stalked over to him with blood dripping from his muzzle.

An urge to protect—to kill—that was so strong it took his breath away, swelled within Kaden until his body was no longer his own. He felt a flush of heat race just beneath his skin, from his scalp to his toes, just before his heart began to beat so fast he thought he might pass out.

He tried to keep his sight fixed on the large wolf baring his fangs at his mate, but a searing, white-hot pain lanced through every inch of his body with an intensity he'd never have thought bearable by one person. Before his stomach could heave its contents as the room span out from underneath him, the pain was replaced with a pleasure that was no less intense in its ferocity.

The pleasure felt deep, abiding, and unquestionably right, as though he was being welcomed into a home that had been calling to him for his entire life. As wonderful as it felt, though, it did not diminish the rage that gripped him over the threat to his mate. Rather, it encouraged and guided him to take the strength and speed he needed to defend what was his.

Without another thought, he closed the space between himself and the menacing wolf in two large bounds and gloried in the blood that began to flow rapidly with each slash of his claws.

"Michael!"

The sharpness of the call through the mental link sent shards of pain piercing into his head, pulling a groan from his lips. He tried to blink his surroundings into focus but needed to give his eyes time to adjust.

"Michael! Get off your ass and tell your mate to calm down."

His mate? That got him going, but as soon as he put his weight on his left wrist to lift himself into a sitting position, the pain drove him back down. He let out a grunt and started cursing, until a wet nose pushed its way into his vision. He rolled over onto his back and was promptly assaulted by a raspy, eager tongue, fur, and whines that filled his ears.

Cradling his injured wrist, he raised the other one to swat the wolf away but it left before he got the chance. To his side, vicious snarls and low growls replaced the whines and he heard another *"Michael!"* boom through his head. When he was finally able to sit up and take in the scene before him, his confusion tripled.

A fine-boned, small white wolf, covered almost completely with blood, was crouched low to the ground in front of him, snapping at anyone in the group of his men that tried to get too close to Michael. There was a much larger brown wolf lying dead in a mass of exposed muscle and blood off to his right, which he recognised as the Alpha he'd been fighting, but he didn't remember making the final blow that had killed him.

When he looked back at the men standing in the doorway, Sam smiled at him hesitantly and asked, "Michael, are you all right?"

Michael ran a quick internal inspection of his body while patting himself down with his good hand. He had a gash running across his stomach and a few more lining his back. There were teeth punctures on the back of his neck and his wrist was broken, but there was nothing that wouldn't heal in a day or so. "Yeah. I think so. What the hell happened?"

He saw his father relax in relief before replying, "I think we can figure that out, but first, why don't you ask your mate to back off just a bit so we can get you out of here?"

Michael furrowed his brow but recognition was almost instant. His mate was the delicate wolf standing over him, protecting him from potential harm.

The pride he felt at that knowledge was quickly dampened as he took in the state of the white were. There was so much blood on Kaden, he couldn't determine how much of it belonged to him or his mate. His fur was thin and even missing in some places—nothing like the thick pelt that should be covering his frail body to prepare him for winter.

"Baby? I'm not in any danger. I need you to come here so I can look you over."

The wolf immediately turned his attention back to him and whined as he slid to his belly and crawled back to Michael. He lightly skimmed his fingers over the fine hairs barely concealing the skin underneath and felt tears forming as he grazed over a multitude of scratches, welts, and teeth marks covering the majority of Kaden's wolf form.

Blinking them back, he asked, "Can you shift back for me, baby?"

The young wolf merely looked him in the eyes before crawling into his lap and collapsing with a barely audible huff.

"Son," Sam spoke up again. "I think we need to get Kaden back home where we can tend his injuries. Do you want me to carry him?"

"No!" he snapped, then cleared his throat and said more quietly, "I'm sorry. I can carry him, but I don't think he can shift back yet. Is there a blanket anywhere I can wrap him in?"

Joseph strode over to a couch several feet away and pulled a thin, cotton blanket from the back of it. He laid it down over the now-sleeping form of the little wolf in Michael's arms, then stepped back as Michael stood up and tucked the material around his mate as gently as possible.

Michael grudgingly gave Kaden over to his father while he dressed. He then took Kaden back and rode with Sam while Nick drove his truck back to his house. His father gave him the details of the fights he'd missed. Joseph had been forced to kill Thomas when the Beta had refused to back down, but Gregory's other two Betas had given up not long after that. A few of their men had suffered minor injuries, but all in all, it seemed to have been a success.

Michael could tell that his father was avoiding the details of Gregory's death, but didn't bother to ask why. He knew he hadn't actually killed the Alpha before he'd been knocked unconscious, but his only concern now was for the small being in his arms.

Katherine and Missy were sitting on the porch steps when they arrived back at Michael's house. The other men had already taken their separate ways home, planning on reconvening in the morning to discuss their next course of action. Sam parked the car and Michael thought he saw one of Kaden's ears twitch but he made no other move. Michael shifted the slight weight in his arms and got out as Sam opened the door for him.

Missy ran towards them with worry written all over her face. "Where's Kaden? Is he okay? You said you would bring him back to me. What happened?"

Sam took her shoulders in a firm grip as she raced past him, before she could plough into Michael in her eagerness to get information. "It's okay, honey. Kaden's right there in the blanket."

Sam pointed to the limp figure in Michael's arms. Missy hesitated for a few seconds before cautiously approaching the form and lowering her nose to the tip of the muzzle peeking out from the cover. She inhaled deeply and a look of profound relief and joy softened her features, making her look even younger and sweeter than she already was. She sent a grateful smile up to Michael, then stepped aside so he could proceed to the front door.

As he walked inside, he heard the girl whisper to Sam, "He's hurt, isn't he? Will he be all right?"

"Yeah. Nothing that some sleep and a few good meals can't fix. Your brother's one tough wolf," Sam replied.

Michael let their voices drift away as he took the stairs as fast as he dared. Once in his bedroom, he closed the door and turned on the bedside lamp, then went straight to the bathroom. Sitting on the edge of the tub, he turned on the water, making sure it wasn't too hot before setting about the task of unravelling his mate from the blanket surrounding him.

The cloth pulled at some of the wounds where dried blood had fused them together but Kaden remained mercifully unconscious. Michael laid Kaden down on the bathroom rug and had divested himself of his clothes by the time the bath was ready.

Slowly, he lowered them both into the soothing water, keeping Kaden's wolf form securely against his chest, and laid back with a sigh.

Ever since awakening to find the small were guarding him, he hadn't felt a flicker of emotion from him. It was a little alarming, but his contentedness over having his mate once again safe and alive in his arms was too overwhelming. He revelled in the soft rhythm of Kaden's breathing and heartbeat and allowed it to lull him into sleep.

Some time later, he became aware of a subtle shifting in the air in front of him and opened his eyes. Two beautiful, violet orbs met his gaze out of a face lit by the soft, yellow lamplight seeping in from the next room. Kaden's expression was carefully schooled and Michael found himself afraid to move, or even breathe, for fear of breaking the connection of this moment and driving the smaller man away.

They continued to stare at each other for countless seconds, but it was not uncomfortable. Michael was prepared to wait an eternity if it meant giving his mate the time he needed to come to terms with all of the events of the past few weeks. Apprehension flitted through his mind but, before he could squelch it, Kaden's lips turned up in a knowing smile. It seemed to break the tension Michael hadn't even been aware of, and he allowed his own features to relax.

"You came for me." The words were no more than a caress on his skin, yet they held a wealth of wonder in them.

"I should never have lost you. I'm so sorry, sweetheart. I never meant..."

"Don't. You saved me. When I saw you fighting Gregory, I wasn't afraid anymore. I felt strong...powerful. And mad."

"You killed him, didn't you?"

Kaden lowered his lids for a second. "I think so. I didn't mean to. I just couldn't stand to watch him hurt you anymore."

A small smile played at Michael's lips as he said, "You were protecting your mate. I saw the damage you did to him, and I'm so proud of you. But I gotta say, between you and Mom, I think I'm a little scared."

Instead of laughing at his attempt to lighten the mood, Kaden seemed to become more anxious. "But...why did you come? I thought... I saw your face after I told you how Gregory used me. I can't change my past. I'll always be an embarrassment to you."

Michael let loose the tight rein with which he'd been holding in his emotions and allowed his guilt to wash over him. He looked down over his mate's slender body, scored by various wounds and bruises, then back up at his face. His silken locks were severely thinned and lacked some of their previous lustre, his eyes ringed with dark circles and his cheeks hollow. The skin that had once been glowing with life was now pale and chilled despite the lingering warmth of the water they were soaking in.

And Michael had never seen a more precious sight.

He placed his hands on Kaden's cheeks and bowed his head until their foreheads were touching. He wanted to lick moisture back into those dry, chapped lips, but it was imperative that he settle all doubts now.

"Kaden, you have never been an embarrassment to me. You were frightening at first, an unknown variable. You took my life and turned it upside down, made me feel things I was unprepared for."

"You're not exactly winning any brownie points here," Kaden grumbled.

Michael chuckled softly and said, "Patience, boy. My point is, I have never been as happy as I have been these past few weeks with you. What Gregory did was my fault. I'm the one who is undeserving of you, and I will do anything to make that up to you. I'll renounce my status as Alpha so I can devote more time to you, I'll get on my knees every morning and beg your forgiveness. I'll..."

Kaden stopped him with a kiss that was as passionate as it was demanding. He took control and swept his tongue into Michael's mouth, delving inside with an urgency that had them both hard and panting before they had to pull apart to catch their breath. And finally, *finally*, Kaden let go of the band on his own emotions and the flood of joy that poured out of him had Michael so aroused his hips jerked up involuntarily.

"You're going to be the death of me," Michael groaned.

"Maybe," Kaden giggled, "but not today."

"I take it you've decided to keep me?"

Kaden squinted one eye and creased his brow. "I don't know yet. Can grovelling come in the form of blow jobs?"

Michael growled and took possession of his lips, taking all of the control this time.

Epilogue

One month later…

Michael stepped out of the shower and grabbed a towel, drying himself off as he hurried into the bedroom, but he was pulled up short by the magnificent sight of his mate standing in front of the dresser mirror. The man was wearing a black tuxedo that showed off every curve and angle of his body to perfection.

The contrast of the colour against his pale skin and platinum hair made the beautiful features of his face stand out boldly. Combined with the slight flush in his cheeks and the fullness of his lips, red from his constant worrying at them, he made the most striking image Michael had ever seen in his life.

"Damn, boy. Have I told you lately how gorgeous you are?"

Kaden's clear, blue-violet gaze met his in the mirror and his mate let out a burst of laughter he knew he would never get enough of. He dropped the towel to the floor and walked towards him, bending down to press his growing cock into the crease of his mate's ass while wrapping his arms around his slender waist.

A moan escaped Kaden's lips and he thrust his hips back wickedly while saying, "Mom's going to kill you if you get me all wrinkled and ruin the hard work she put into making this suit."

Michael leaned his head down and chuckled into his mate's ear before licking his tongue along the inside curve. "The ceremony doesn't start for another twenty minutes, and I think mom would rather see you wrinkled than watch me walk around our guests with a hard-on all day."

Kaden span around and wrapped his hands behind Michael's neck before jumping up and twining his legs around his waist. He could feel the man's already solid length grind against his stomach and the heated look in those huge, sultry eyes almost had him coming right then.

"I guess we should take care of that now then, shouldn't we?"

Before Michael could respond, his mate jumped back out of his arms and dropped to his knees, looking up at him through his thick lashes before opening his mouth and taking his cock to the back of his throat in one fluid movement.

The sensation of Kaden's throat muscles swallowing convulsively around the head was so sudden that he almost shouted in pleasure as he leant forward to grip the edge of the dresser behind his mate's head. This only succeeded in pushing his cock further into the sweet mouth wrapped around it. He was about to pull up when Kaden stopped him by reaching his hands up to cup Michael's ass and massage his cheeks.

Michael could only brace himself and watch as his mate sucked in as he slowly pulled back, biting down softly as he reached the skin just behind the head, pulling a hiss and an involuntary thrust from him. In torturously lazy circles, Kaden slid the flat of his tongue around the sensitive area, using the pressure of his lips and the suction of his mouth to coax several drops of pre-cum from him. Kaden lapped them up greedily, flicking the tip of his tongue across the slit before engulfing his entire length again into the hot cavern of his mouth.

Watching the joy in his lover's eyes as he took control of their lovemaking was nearly as sensual as the talent of his tongue and lips. As Kaden pulled back again with a soft moan, the vibrations of his throat shot through his cock and his eyes rolled back in ecstasy.

"You're killing me, boy," he ground out as he reached down to gently strip the brilliant blond locks from his mate's face. The man's answering chuckle sent frissons of pleasure racing up his thighs and straight to his groin. It was more than he could take, and he began to pump his hips forward in a fast rhythm that had Kaden tightening the hold on his ass to keep his balance.

After only seconds, he felt the tingling sensation that presaged his orgasm race down his spine and had to pull out of his mate's talented mouth, grinding through his teeth, "Strip, boy, while I can still control my actions."

Kaden obeyed him immediately, not able to keep the huge grin from his face. He threw his clothes in all directions, then jumped to the middle of the bed on his hands and knees and wiggled his perfect little behind in front of him. Michael was about to reach for the drawer of the nightstand that held the lube when he noticed something protruding from Kaden's ass.

"Is that a...?" Michael was just about to ask his mate when the hell—and *where* the hell—he had bought a butt plug, but his mate beat him to it.

Kaden span around again and began bouncing in his excitement. "It's a mating present from Nick. I've never used one before, but he told me how to..."

"Nick did *what?*" Michael practically shouted.

He was going to kill him. Plain and simple. But very, very painfully.

Kaden's laugh was high and carefree. "Oh please. It's not like he *showed* me." Michael let out a low growl but his mate merely laughed again and swung back around. "I'm all ready for you, now fuck me before I burst. Please!"

Okay, he could kill Nick later. When his mate begged like that, it was his undoing every time. He climbed onto the bed and bent the top half of his body over Kaden's back, kissing his way up and nipping him gently around his ribs. Kaden giggled until he swept his tongue along his spine, taking the time to dip into the shallows around his neck.

His boy shivered as Michael licked his way to Kaden's ear and asked, "So did Nick tell you about everything this little baby can do?" He reached down to grasp the edges of the plug and pushed it in further while slowly moving it up and down.

He knew that he'd found his gland when Kaden nearly jumped forward with a surprised cry.

"Oh, no you don't. You wanted to play. Now it's my turn." Michael pushed Kaden's head down until it rested on the mattress then wrapped his arm around his narrow hips, continuing his manipulation of the plug in his ass. He could feel his mate start to tremble as little whimpers flew from his lips every time he slid the plug over his nub. He breathed in the sweet, floral scent of his mate's pre-cum and felt his own cock dripping in anticipation.

"Oh, oh, Michael, p—please. I need more. I need you..."

Michael knew his mate was close and his slow torture only made his own rock-hard erection more painful by the second. He pulled the plug out and drove himself in to the hilt in one smooth movement, not giving Kaden time to adjust.

They both cried out at the intense pleasure but Michael couldn't stop. The lube already coating his boy's inner walls allowed him to glide in easily, building up friction until all he could feel was the warmth and tightness of Kaden's ass.

He held his hips in a bruising grip and pounded into him over and over again. The cries of pleasure from his mate only spurred him on to go harder, faster, and he could feel his orgasm coming on strongly as his balls tightened to near pain. He angled Kaden's back downwards, forcing him to point his ass even higher into the air.

He'd long ago given up trying to distinguish his own feelings of ecstasy and rapture from those of his mate. They twined like ribbons around both of them until nothing else existed but them and this one moment in time.

When Kaden screamed his name and the walls of his sweet hole clamped down on him convulsively, he knew his mate had found his release. The pleasure that came from it increased his own impossibly and he slammed himself in once, twice more before giving in to a rush so great that he thought he might fly apart.

He kept Kaden locked in his embrace as his cock pulsed inside him, filling him completely. The satisfaction he felt every time they made love was both everything and never enough. He was quickly becoming a sex fiend and loving every minute of it.

Finally, he toppled to the side and pulled himself out with a grunt, turning his boy in his arms so that he could stare into those eyes that made him feel like the most important person in the world. The most cherished and loved—and he hoped that his eyes reflected the same.

It took them long minutes to slow their breathing and, of course, his pup was the first to recover.

"Soo…" he drawled, "how mad do you think Mom's going to be when we show up ten minutes late?"

Michael let out a bark of laughter and smoothed back the shining strands of his mate's hair. It was still very thin, but it glowed brighter than the brilliant beams of the moon across the still, black waters of a lake under a clear night sky.

Beautiful.

"We'll blame it on Nick and his wonderful gift." The burst of happiness that came from Kaden shot through him like lightning as the man released another peal of laughter so amazing, it caught his breath in his throat.

"Come on, mate. Clean me up." Kaden pulled him from the bed and led him into the bathroom, where they got into the shower together. They took their time washing each other thoroughly, enjoying the way their emotions bounced from one to the other. The moment they stepped out, a loud knock on the door ended their intentions of holding off the party for another twenty minutes.

"Don't make me come in there after you boys. Neither one of you has anything I haven't seen before, so if you think your bare butts are going to put me off, think again," Katherine yelled through the door. "And if I see one wrinkle in the suits I made for both of you, I'll haunt you after I die!"

Kaden laughed again, so loudly that Michael had to kiss him to cut off his outburst. He growled against his lips, "She may love you too much to kill you, but I don't think I'd be that lucky. Now shut up and get your sexy ass back in your suit so we can go." He broke off the kiss and smacked his mate's delectable backside before going to the closet to retrieve his own outfit.

He slipped on his suit quickly and made sure that he was at the door to their bedroom before Kaden eventually managed to pull himself away from his reflection in the dresser mirror to proclaim that he was ready.

Some may call that vanity, but it had taken him more than two weeks to convince his mate that the reflected image he saw in the mirror was one that Michael adored more than anything else in his life. And so, his boy primped and preened just for him. And he enjoyed every moment of watching him learn to love the person he was, inside and out.

When Kaden skipped to him and bounced on the balls of his feet, barely able to contain his happiness,

Michael grinned and had to press down on his shoulders to keep him still.

"Slow down there, pup. There's something that I want to ask you before we go to our celebration."

Kaden's face instantly dropped its mirth and his emotions of worry and fear lanced through Michael's chest like knives tearing at his heart. "No, baby. Please don't worry." He pulled a small, flat box from his left jacket pocket and awkwardly pressed it into Kaden's hand. "I know you like it out at Henry's ranch, and now that you can take wolf form, it's easy for you to travel back and forth…"

Kaden snorted. "Don't you mean us? You haven't let me travel alone once since I started training the horses again."

Michael narrowed his eyes in mock offence at the interruption but only got a smirk for his effort.

"As I was saying, I was wondering if I could talk you into staying here. Working here." He held up his hand at the protest about to jump from his mate's mouth. "The guys and I have already started plans to build a stable and corral behind the house after we relocate some of the trees in that area.

"Henry agreed to let you transport the horses you're currently working with so that you can train them here. 'Course you'll have to take Missy with you. Mrs Connel threatened me in no uncertain terms that our lives would be at stake if we didn't bring your sister to visit. Henry also said he knows of a few other ranchers that would appreciate your services."

Michael reached to the almost-forgotten box in the man's hand and opened it, pulling out a large Ford key. "And this is the key to a truck with a trailer already attached so that you can drive the horses back and forth from the ranches. All I need to know is if you're okay with this."

Kaden stood with his jaw open, eyes bulging, for so long that Michael was starting to get nervous. He wanted to touch him but had to know that whatever answer the boy gave was made in honesty, without his influence.

"Baby?"

"That's way too much. I can't let you do that."

"That's not what I asked. If I do set everything up, will you stay here with me? Train them here?"

"Well yeah, but..."

Michael swept him up in a fierce hug, squeezing the next protest out of him. "Please accept this, because I need you. I love you, for everything that you are. My heart, my salvation, my mate."

Kaden sighed and melted into him. "Yes, and I love you, too."

About the Author

I have always been a lover of books, particularly those with the dichotomy of the strong alpha male and the weaker love of their life which they must rescue. After reading all I could find in M/F books, I decided to give M/M fiction a try and my addiction skyrocketed.

Hot, sexy men times two? No contest. Unfortunately, I was reading faster than the authors could produce. Eventually, I resorted to imagining my own stories and my mind took off from there.

I have to admit, though, I am a bit of a recluse. If not for the joy and humour my husband and four boys bring to me, I would never have ventured this far.

Nikki McCoy loves to hear from readers.

You can find her contact information, website details and author profile page at http://www.total-e-bound.com.

Total-E-Bound Publishing

www.total-e-bound.com

Take a look at our exciting range of literagasmic™
erotic romance titles and discover pure quality
at Total-E-Bound.

www.ingramcontent.com/pod-product-compliance
Lightning Source LLC
Chambersburg PA
CBHW030144180626
46812CB00002B/840